The EIGHTY-FIVE BILLION EUROMAN

The EIGHTY-FIVE BILLION EURO MAN

DONAL CONATY

First published in 2011 by Y Books
Lucan, Co. Dublin
Ireland
Tel & Fax: +353 1 621 7992
publishing@ybooks.ie
www.ybooks.ie

Text © 2011 Donal Conaty
Editing, design and layout © 2011 Y Books

Paperback   ISBN: 978-1-908023-18-6
Ebook - Mobi format   ISBN: 978-1-908023-19-3
Ebook - epub format   ISBN: 978-1-908023-20-9

A CIP catalogue record for this book is available from the British Library.

10 9 8 7 6 5 4 3 2 1

Typeset in New Caledonia LT Std 12/18pt

Typeset by Y Books
Cover design by Graham Thew Design
Front cover illustration by Alan Clarke
Printed and bound by CPI Mackays, Chatham ME5 8TD

Contents

☆ ☆ ☆ ☆ ☆ ☆ ☆ ☆

Biography
✩ ✩ ✩ ✩ ✩ ✩ ✩ ✩ ✩ ✩

Donal Conaty has worked as a journalist in Dublin and London. He now lives in Sligo where he writes and publishes the online satirical journal, *The Mire*. www.themire.net

DEDICATION
✫✫✫✫✫✫✫✫✫✫

For Anna, Laoise and Ríáin

ACKNOWLEDGEMENTS

☆☆☆☆☆☆☆☆☆☆☆☆☆☆☆

This book would not have been possible were it not for the good work of Ajai Chopra and his colleagues in the IMF, EU and ECB. We shall never be able to repay your generosity.

I would like to thank Brian Cowen, Brian Lenihan and Mary Coughlan for their boundless enthusiasm in inspiring this book. Similar gratitude is also due to Taoiseach Enda Kenny, Minister for Finance Michael Noonan, Minister for Public Expenditure and Reform Brendan Howlin, Minister for Social Protection Joan Burton and Minister for Transport, Tourism and Sport Leo Varadkar for services to comedy. A nod also goes to Luke 'Ming' Flanagan, Mick Wallace, Mary O'Rourke and Joe Higgins. And I mustn't forget Mary Harney and Bertie Ahern.

Sean FitzPatrick, Michael Fingleton and sundry other bankers are also due a debt of gratitude. Thank you, gentlemen, thank you.

Mere words cannot express my gratitude to Ireland's senior civil servants. Heroic is what you are!

Sincere thanks to Robert Doran and Chenile Keogh of Y Books for seeing the opportunity for this book and for having the nerve to go for it. Thanks too for their patience while it was being written. Particular thanks to Robert for his excellent work in editing the book. Thanks also to Alan Clarke for the excellent cover illustration, Kieran Kelly for his legal expertise and to Natasha Mac a'Bháird for the proofread.

This book grew out of the *@IMFDublinDiary* Twitter feed and stories I wrote for my online journal, *The Mire* (www.themire.net). Thank you to the readers and followers of *The Mire*, *@IMFDublinDiary* and *@themiredotnet* on Twitter.

Thanks to Eoin Purcell of *Irish Publishing News* who was quick to see the potential of *@IMFDublinDiary*.

Special thanks to Daragh Fallon, Dessie McFadden, Oisin Horler, Dec Bruen, Colin Gillen and The Grange Players for helping with *The Mire*. Thanks too to Dermot Healy and the Dooneel Writing Group.

Writing a book in a few short months when you are used to writing stories four paragraphs long creates its own tensions. Thanks to my wife Anna and my children Laoise and Ríáin for indulging me in this and at other times.

Thanks also to those people, too numerous to mention, who have lent me money and bought me drinks over the years. Now would not be a good time to stop.

'The boom times are getting even more boomier.'
BERTIE AHERN, JULY 2006

✪

'[This is] the cheapest bailout in the world so far.'
BRIAN LENIHAN, OCTOBER 2008

✪

'We are not rushing into the banks without knowing
precisely what the position is in those banks.'
BRIAN LENIHAN, NOVEMBER 2008

✪

'Let's be fair about it – we all partied.'
BRIAN LENIHAN, NOVEMBER 2010

✪

'Ireland has made no application for external support.'
BRIAN COWEN, NOVEMBER 2010

✪

'Paddy likes to know what the story is.'
ENDA KENNY, FEBRUARY 2011

'We will not put any more money into Irish banks that do not come up with a credible plan to debt share with the bondholders, not one red cent.'
LEO VARADKAR, FEBRUARY 2011

'All politicians are spoofers.'
MICHAEL NOONAN, FEBRUARY 2011

'This programme is a lifeline for Ireland. It represents an Irish solution to an Irish problem.'
AJAI CHOPRA, APRIL 2011

DISCLAIMER
☆ ☆ ☆ ☆ ☆ ☆ ☆ ☆ ☆

This book is a work of fiction. It is also intended to be a work of humour and satire. None of the scenes described in this book have occurred. All characters who feature in the book, other than the politicians and well-known public representatives, are entirely imaginary and do not have any relationship to or foundation in any real persons. The thoughts, words and deeds attributed to all the characters in the book derive entirely from the author's imagination.

ONE

Ajai Has Landed

☆ ☆

It was typical of Ajai to brief us on the mission mid-flight. He just loves *Criminal Minds*.

We were sitting around the table digesting figures on the Irish banking and public finances crisis. Ajai handed out photos and short text profiles of the key figures involved.

'As you know, we're going to Ireland,' he said. 'This shouldn't be the most difficult situation we've ever faced.'

We all agreed with him. How little we knew then.

'Ten years ago the Irish inadvertently created a booming economy,' Ajai continued. 'Like many before them they thought it would last forever. It didn't. The economy collapsed four years ago and the Irish only realised it when the global financial crisis kicked in. They were still trying to sell the notion of a soft landing a full twelve months after their economy had crashed and burned.

'On the one hand this is straightforward – we have to get them to cut back on public spending. A lot of jobs will have to go. During the so-called boom years every civil servant was given a civil servant. Importantly, their public service must also be seen to adjust, because the general population has already done so. A lot of Irish people thought they'd won the lottery without even buying a ticket. That's over and they know it. These people have had to rethink their lives. Their short- to medium-term future is high taxes, high unemployment and high emigration. The days of luxury living that some of them enjoyed are over.

'On the other hand there's the banking crisis. Again, this should be straightforward. They should default, but Europe will fall like a house of cards if they do. So we have to cosy along with the ECB and pretend we think the Irish people should honour their banks' debts, for the moment at least.

'Our mission is to make sure the situation doesn't worsen and that they learn a lesson here. We need to introduce a sensible, prudent culture in their Department of Finance.'

Ajai looked directly at me.

'You're Irish, right?' he asked.

I looked up. 'Great-great-grandparents on both sides left Ireland during the Famine,' I said. 'The Great Hunger they called it. I'm as Irish as a pint of Guinness.'

'Actually, Guinness is owned by a French company. So technically you'd have to be as French as Guinness.' IMF whiz kid Nelson Coontz may have been a fully qualified actuary at the age of five but sometimes he could be a real pain in the ass.

'Hey, I'm proud to be Irish. Watch what you're saying.'

Ajai raised a hand to calm us and showed me the most airbrushed photograph of any man I had ever seen. I shrugged, not recognising him.

'Is he any relation to Silvio Berlusconi?' I asked.

'Let's hope not. That's Dermot Mulhearn, Chief of Staff of the Irish Department of Finance. Good relations with him are critical to the success of this project,' Ajai said.

'What about this guy?' I held up a photo of a man with heavily dyed unnaturally-black hair.

'That's the Minister for Finance, Brian Lenihan,' Ajai said. 'Be polite but try not to get cornered by him. I met him in a lift in Brussels once and it took me two hours to get away from him. He is a fervent believer in whatever he happens to be saying, even if he's reading it for the first time.

'You should treat any government politicians you meet with a degree of respect. But don't waste time on them. Look at these two.' Ajai waved headshots of two mundane looking middle-aged men in the air. 'Dempsey and Ahern,' he said. 'Two of the most senior ministers in the Irish government. Two days ago they denied all knowledge that the IMF was coming to Ireland. These guys could meet us at the airport and tell us we're not there. The main thing to remember is that these politicians are just clinging to power for the next few months. The civil service is the key to this. Politicians come and go.'

'What about the opposition?' I asked.

Ajai permitted himself a rare smile.

'Same thing applies. Again, be polite but don't waste time on them,' he said.

He held up another photo. 'This is the leader of the opposition and very probably the leader of the next Irish Government,' he said. 'Whenever the economy is mentioned his handlers send him to the corner shop for an ice cream. If you have to deal with him give him an errand to do. Apparently he's very biddable. I'm told he's compulsive about tidiness, so if all else fails get him to polish something shiny or clean the windows. It seems to work for his handlers.

'So, are we clear that Mulhearn is our man? If we are to get Ireland living within its means, he is the one we have to convince.'

I studied the photograph of Mulhearn. It could have been issued by a Hollywood studio. He wasn't an old man, early forties I would guess, but he was clearly a fan of botox and sunbeds. His dyed-black eyebrows were in stark contrast to the burnt-orange colour of his face. His Italian-looking shoes were burnt orange too, as was the silk handkerchief in the breast pocket of his navy suit. The photograph showed him sitting on his desk. An elaborate chandelier was reflected in the shiny leather of his shoes, and there was something about his suit. I held the photograph up to the light.

'Is that real gold thread on his suit collar?' I asked.

'Yes,' said Ajai. 'I admit he might need some convincing.'

When we arrived at Dublin Airport there was nothing to suggest a country in collapse. We were ushered through a magnificently opulent and utterly empty terminal. It had opened just the previous week, apparently. I shouldn't think they will be building any more of them. 'Look at this!' Ajai said. 'They built a brand new terminal for their people to emigrate from.' Like all of us, Ajai hates waste. It goes with the job.

We emerged into some confusion at arrivals. Airport staff, who clearly had nothing to do, and a few business travellers gathered around us.

'Thank God you're here,' said a businessman, grabbing my hand and shaking it vigorously. 'We thought you'd never come.'

'We've been expecting you for months,' a woman in an Aer Lingus uniform said. 'What took you so long?' She held Ajai's hands in hers for what seemed like an eternity. 'Count your fingers before you leave,' she said. 'They'll take everything you have, everything.'

Ajai broke away from her grip and we continued somewhat uneasily towards the exit. We were taken aback to find uniformed chauffeurs waiting outside the terminal for each of us. Ajai was furious at this extravagance but he told us to go with our drivers and meet at the hotel. Now that they were here they would have to be paid anyway.

My car, limousine really, was usually at the disposal of the Minister for Finance, the driver told me. It was beautifully finished in walnut and leather and came with … someone's shopping.

'Whose are these?' I asked the driver, indicating the paper bags from a store called Brown Thomas.

'They're yours!' he said cheerily. 'A small welcome gift from the Irish people to our friends in the IMF.'

I examined the contents of some of the bags. An Xbox Kinect with 250 GB console, an iPhone 4, a Kindle *and* a Sony Reader. This was extraordinary. And there were clothes, lots of designer clothes in my size and with my initials embroidered on them. You wouldn't get such extravagant goodie bags at the Oscars. An A4 envelope contained a Certificate of Irishness and a brief note from the Chief of Staff at the Department of Finance, Dermot Mulhearn. 'Welcome home' it said simply.

'I can't accept this stuff,' I said.

I could feel the driver sizing me up in the rearview mirror.

'I suppose I could take the Xbox off your hands if you don't want it,' he said tentatively.

'Want it? I don't want any of it. It has to go back to be refunded. This can't be paid for by the taxpayer.'

I watched him roll his eyes heavenwards. 'I pay tax,' he said. 'Sometimes, anyway. I don't mind you having them. Sure aren't you one of our own?'

When we arrived at the Merrion Hotel in central Dublin, Ajai and the rest of the team confirmed that they too had been given goodie bags. 'Our Xbox consoles are only 4 GB though. They must like you,' Ajai observed. 'I guess they know you're Irish. We might be able to use that.' Ajai dismissed our drivers and phoned the Department of Finance to make sure nothing like that happened again. 'OK guys, check into your rooms and meet in the lobby in ten minutes,' he told us. 'We're going to walk to work.'

When you travel as much as we do you tend not to notice the hotels. One blurs into another. We're not looking for a room with a view, and we're generally just happy if it has working powerpoints, wifi and a trouser press. The Merrion Hotel had all that and then some. 'Gracious Irish living' is what they pride themselves on, or so the headed paper said. It was all chandeliers and Italian marble floors – a far cry from the Holiday Inn we stayed at in Athens. The Department of Finance had booked our rooms and they had gone over the top. There was champagne waiting for me in my suite, along with some handmade Irish chocolates and a complimentary Department of Finance bathrobe hung in the Jacuzzi-equipped bathroom.

Ten minutes later as we walked across the road to work, I reflected on our journey in from the airport. I guess we never visit a country that doesn't have problems, but at first glance Ireland didn't seem to have too many. We didn't need armed guards and there were no queues of desperate people at cash machines withdrawing their savings. However, there were homeless people at every cash machine. This struck me as strange in a country that according to our briefing documents has tens of thousands of empty houses. 'They're already used to seeing beggars on the street. That's no bad thing,' Ajai observed brightly.

We were greeted at the Department of Finance by a row of dignitaries. All the senior government ministers were there. I knew Dempsey and Ahern from the photographs Ajai had showed us during the flight. They were too caught up in the game of Rock, Paper, Scissors they were playing to notice our arrival, however. Ministerial cars were double-parked on the street causing traffic chaos. I recognised my driver from earlier and acknowledged him but he stared right through me. Guess he had his heart set on that Xbox.

First we were introduced to a churlish, grumpy man who everyone called Taoiseach. An aide told us that Taoiseach was Irish for Prime Minister. I think this was my first experience of the famous Irish sense of humour at work. Whoever he was, they got rid of him quickly. 'I'll catch ye later for a pint,' he called over his shoulder as he was ushered away. 'I can't be idly chatting to the IMF. Pat Carey is announcing a vital Irish language initiative.'

We were finally introduced to Dermot Mulhearn. 'You'll meet the Taoiseach some night during the week,' he assured us. 'He's not really a morning person.' Mulhearn was clearly the man in charge – he had a certain aura, like he was in higher definition to his compatriots. Even the Finance Minister, an intense, slightly manic man, deferred to him.

'You are very welcome, gentlemen,' the Minister began, 'I've read all your books, Mr Chopra. Perhaps you would do me the great honour of signing them?'

'I think you're referring to Deepak Chopra,' Ajai told him with a grimace as he looked at the pile of paperbacks the Minister was holding.

'I'll take it from here, Minister,' Dermot interrupted. 'Why don't you have a read of the sports pages?' He handed

him a newspaper. 'Don't read the news section though –
you'll only upset yourself.'

Everything about Dermot was richer than those around
him. He looked like a 3D version of the airbrushed photograph Ajai showed me on the plane. The man towered over
us. He was maybe 6 ft 2" but he held himself taller. His manner was disconcertingly informal.

'Ajai,' he said, gripping the boss by both shoulders. 'It's
good of you to come in our hour of need. We are like yourselves now – a third world country.'

Ajai removed Dermot's hands from his shoulders and
stepped back slightly.

'If you are referring to India, Mr Mulhearn, I would
respectfully suggest that its finances are in much better
shape than yours.'

'Indeed,' said Dermot, smiling broadly.

I would get used to him saying 'indeed' every time he
wanted to end a conversation.

We walked on plush carpeting through halls hung with
portraits of former finance ministers. From the antique
lamps on the desks to the polished Georgian door handles,
everything suggested grandeur and high office. Eventually,
Dermot showed us to a room with a few free desks. 'This is
your base,' he said. 'Make yourselves at home.' Then Dermot
and Ajai went for a private meeting while we got settled in.
As I was arranging my calculators on my new desk, I noticed
a pensioner lady standing in the doorway.

'Have any of you lads seen my nephew?' she asked.

'Your nephew?' I said, puzzled – it seemed a strange

question. 'Are you sure you are in the right place? This is the Department of Finance.'

'Of course it is, you silly goose,' she said. 'He's the Minister for Finance. You must be new here, are you?'

'Just arrived this morning Ma'am,' I said.

'Don't call me Ma'am,' she retorted, seemingly pointlessly. 'Oh I know, you must be one of the IMF lads. I suppose you've met Dermot, have you? You poor boy. Now where is my nephew? I have to bring him shopping for a suit, or he'll never be leader.'

'I saw him about twenty minutes ago. He was reading a newspaper when we came in.'

'A newspaper? Oh, God save us! He'll have taken that to the toilet with him. He could be gone for hours,' she said as she left.

I spent the rest of the day drilling down through figures provided by Dermot's colleagues. I noticed that the Department of Finance seemed to have spent extraordinary sums on financial consultants, with one in particular drawing six-figure sums every month. I resolved to get to the bottom of it with Dermot the next day.

Back at the hotel later that evening, we had a debriefing session with Ajai. He decided that he would handle the politicians and other stakeholders for the following few days. I was given the task of negotiating with Dermot, and the rest of the team were to do due diligence on the figures.

Ajai asked me what I thought of our first day in Ireland.

'I have to say the Irish negotiators have been very generous. They won't let us put our hands in our pockets for anything. Coffee, lunch, you name it,' I said.

'That's what I'm afraid of,' Ajai said in his usual serious tone. 'They do love to spend money, but they will be spending our money now.'

We turned in early; the flight had taken it out of us. I'll tell you something for nothing – it is great to be working in a developed country for a change. They have a far better quality of mattress in their hotels.

I had a marvellous sleep and was outside the Department of Finance at 6 a.m., reporting for duty. I was still outside at 7, 8 and 9 a.m. Eventually a security guard let me in at 9.45 a.m., after I offered him €20. He insisted he wasn't supposed to let anyone in before 10 a.m. As soon as Dermot arrived, which was shortly before lunch, I asked him about the financial consultancy that was earning a packet from the Department according to the accounts.

'Which one?' Dermot asked.

'Mystic Meg Ltd,' I read from my notes.

Dermot flew into an impressive rage, his skin turning from its normal orange colour to a blood-red and then a threatening purple. 'That bloody woman,' he said blackly. 'She is responsible for all our bad luck.'

'Please explain,' I said. 'How could that be possible?'

He said he'd fill me in over lunch.

'Oh, Minister,' he shouted suddenly. The Finance Minister had put his head around the door.

'Did you want me, Dermot?' he asked with great diffidence.

'I want you to book me a table for two at l'Ecrivain. And

you're not one of the two so don't be getting all excited, Minister,' said Dermot.

We were shown to Dermot's usual table in l'Ecrivain. He seemed to be very well known there. I asked for the set menu but Dermot wouldn't hear of it. 'Let the Irish Government buy you this,' he said. 'It's not often we get one of our Wild Geese back.'

I asked him again about Mystic Meg and he shook his head sadly.

'She ruined us,' he lamented. 'She promised there'd be continued growth and a soft landing. She never prepared us for any of this.'

'Well, a lot of economists thought that,' I said.

'Economists?' he spat the word out. 'Who listens to economists?'

Dermot excused himself to go to the bathroom. Talking about Mystic Meg made him feel sick, he said. Oddly enough he still had an appetite for a foie gras starter and lobster main course.

On his return I asked him what Mystic Meg's credentials were. He put his head in his hands.

'She was very impressive at first,' he said. 'She told my sister she would meet a handsome stranger, and she was spot on. She even introduced them come to think of it.'

'Oh,' I said. I couldn't hide my confusion. 'What exactly

has she done for the Department of Finance?'

'Everything,' he said. 'She's been entirely responsible for economic policy since 2002. Do we have to talk about her? I'm bored.'

I was almost speechless.

'So what was your job?' I asked him.

'My job?' he said. 'My job was to phone her, of course.'

My wild Wicklow venison was going cold as I stared at this man in disbelief. I could not think of anything to say. Could we really train him to take charge of the Irish economy? While I gathered my thoughts, we were interrupted by several officials from other government departments asking Dermot for rugby tickets. He seemed to have any number of tickets and perked up while he exchanged banter with them about the forthcoming match. When they left, Dermot was first to break the silence.

'We thought about suing her,' he said, 'but she strongly advised us against it.'

'What will you do?' I asked weakly.

'Oh, I don't know,' he said. 'I guess I was hoping you'd sort everything out. We could always try phoning Irish Psychics Live. But I'm not sure they're *real* psychics.'

Two hours into the longest lunch I've ever eaten, Dermot started crying into his Calvados Age Inconnu.

'Please, please don't,' he sobbed, grabbing my hands across the table.

'Don't what?' I asked, feeling increasingly uncomfortable.

'Please don't give our money to the Portuguese. They

have the sun,' he said. 'We have nothing.'

I tried to explain to him that that is not how an IMF bailout works, but he was inconsolable as he ordered another Calvados.

☆   ☆   ☆

Ajai raised his eyebrows when I came back to the office after the three-hour lunch break. He summoned me over for a private word at the water cooler.

'We will be having intense negotiations through the weekend,' he said. 'Where's the Irish negotiator?'

'Apparently he is not in the habit of coming back to the office after lunch on a Friday,' I told him nervously.

Ajai pursed his lips; somewhere a president wept.

'How are we supposed to negotiate the Irish bailout without the Irish?' he asked, reasonably enough.

'To be honest, Mr Chopra, I don't think the Irish are that interested in the negotiations. Dermot was going home to get ready for something called the *Toy Show* on television. He was very excited about it.'

Ajai rubbed his temples; somewhere a finance minister had an anxiety attack.

'Right, we'll wait till tomorrow,' he said with an exhausted sigh. 'But if the Irish guys don't show up, you're going to have to negotiate for them.'

I asked Ajai how he had got on with the unions.

'They just wanted pens with IMF written on them,' he

said. 'When we ran out of pens, they lost interest in us and started fighting amongst themselves.'

That evening I shared a sandwich with Ajai in the hotel lobby before we retired for the night. We split the bill between us. Ajai went to bed but I was restless and decided to go for a short walk before bed. Quite near the hotel I came across an impressive monument to Wolfe Tone and I was hit by a sudden nostalgic memory of the stories my dad told me when I was growing up in Jersey about Irish rebel heroes. What would they make of this situation? I walked back to the hotel and turned in for the night.

I woke in the middle of the night to the unsettling sensation that there was someone in my hotel bedroom. And there was. A skinny guy wearing a Christmas jumper was sitting on the end of my bed talking animatedly to Dermot. Who was he? Why were they here? And why on earth was he wearing a Christmas jumper in November?

'What? Who? How did you get in here?' I asked.

'With the key, of course,' Dermot replied with effort-less, inebriated charm. 'We were just on our way to La Cave and were wondering if you would care to join us. How did the old negotiations go anyway? Are we all good? Done and dusted?'

'You weren't there,' I said. 'Ajai postponed them until tomorrow. We can't negotiate with someone who isn't there. It's not how we do things.'

Dermot was clearly put out by this.

'You're after embarrassing me in front of Ryan,' he said.

'Hello Ryan,' I said weakly. 'Welcome to my hotel room.'

Whoever he was, he clearly thought I meant it. The two of them raided the mini-bar and stayed for hours. I had a soda water. I fell asleep listening to the skinny guy going on and on and on about JFK. Another dead Irish hero.

When I woke they were gone and so were my shirts. Damn. I had only met Dermot and I was already exasperated with him. It was like dealing with a disruptive child. They had obviously been amused by the idea of leaving me with just a Shrek goodie bag and an Irish soccer jersey. I tried the jersey on and looked, grim-faced, at my reflection in the mirror. I had to go in and face Ajai on a crucial day for the negotiations wearing an Irish soccer jersey that was three sizes too big for me. I'd rather be waterboarded.

Ajai said nothing when he saw me. We were only in the country a couple of days, but already the most unlikely situations seemed commonplace to him. He reached into his desk drawer and handed me a fresh white shirt. 'Give it back pressed,' he instructed. 'Buy shirts at lunchtime; add them to the bottom line.'

Just as I got up to go, he called me back. 'While you're out, pick up some t-shirts with I ♥ IMF printed on them. Make sure they're XXL. They might be useful during negotiations.'

Dermot was in sparkling form that morning when he led his team into the historic negotiations with us. I have to say he cut an impressive figure in a bespoke three-piece suit, and he certainly didn't look like a man who had been up all night. However, he and his colleagues found it hard to settle into serious discussions. They appeared to be distracted by something.

'This won't take long, will it?' Dermot asked. 'Only we have an important march to go on.'

'Surely you don't mean the march against the Government and the IMF,' said Ajai, shocked.

'Why not?' said Dermot. 'Aren't we all in this together? On the one road sharing the one road and all that.'

Ajai was incredulous.

'But ... you ... are ... the ... Government.' He said each word slowly and deliberately, hoping they would somehow penetrate Dermot's consciousness.

Dermot looked at him with a twinkle in his eye.

'Are we?' he said, 'Or are you? And does anyone really care?' he asked, clearly feeling that the question was rhetorical. He looked at his watch. 'Must go,' he said. 'The march is starting at midday. We can't let the people down. They look to us for leadership. We have to show a bit of solidarity.'

After Dermot left, I tried to persuade Ajai that we could actually get some real work done while the Irish negotiators marched against their Government, but he was concerned about the optics.

'We can't sell this deal if people think the Irish didn't even enter negotiations,' he said. 'We're going to have to play it their way.'

I didn't know what he was going to say next, but I knew I wouldn't like it.

'The Irish negotiators like you,' he said to me. 'You have to help them negotiate a deal they can stick to. It needs to be something they can sell to their people. There's no point, otherwise.'

My heart sank.

'I want you to go after them and join them on the march,' Ajai said. 'And wear this.' He threw me the Irish soccer jersey.

Dermot was as happy as a kid in a candy store when I caught up with them. He threw his arm around me. 'You're one of us now,' he said.

Ajai had warned me about this. 'They say here that the Vikings became more Irish than the Irish themselves,' he had said. 'Don't do that. It would be no help to anybody.'

☆ ☆ ☆

Thousands of people had gathered to protest and I can't say I blamed them. Their country was in disarray and the political leadership seemed hopelessly inadequate. But the marchers were in good humour, cheerfully defiant.

'I've never protested before. It's kind of fun,' I said under my breath to Dermot. But he was distracted. All the

Irish negotiators were passing around Nurofen Plus tablets and using energy drinks to wash them down.

'Want some?' Dermot asked.

'No, I don't have a headache,' I said.

'Take some anyway,' Dermot insisted and handed me two.

I shrugged and swallowed them. Why they all have headaches I don't know. They take enough screen breaks.

It was true that I had never marched in anger or solidarity and I was surprised when I quite liked it. Ordinary people marching for their jobs, their pensions – there was nothing wrong with that. I felt for them. And the crowd continued to be cheerful even as it grew in number.

By contrast, the negotiators from the Department of Finance were becoming boisterous and aggressive. Dermot puffed up his chest when he spotted a group of people he knew. I recognised some of them from lunch at l'Ecrivain the previous day, but they were no longer friendly and affable as they had been on that occasion.

'It's the Department of Justice boys,' Dermot hissed. 'They think they're the No. 1 firm in the country but we'll show them. No one tells us Finance men what to do. Come on!' he roared.

After that, it all happened very quickly. We were suddenly chasing the civil servants from the Department of Justice down a series of side streets until they found themselves in a cul-de-sac and were forced to turn and face us. Cornered, they bunched together and charged straight at us. I saw Dermot go down under a flurry of punches. They closed in on him and started kicking him on the ground. Before I realised what I was doing, I had picked up a corrugated bin and charged at them. They fell away from Dermot and I rounded on the biggest of them – a man who only yesterday had accepted two premium tickets to the rugby from Dermot in l'Ecrivain. Two quick punches to the head and one to the gut put him on the ground. I looked for the next person to hit but they were scurrying away to lick their wounds.

I helped Dermot up. Remarkably, he was completely unharmed.

'We showed those Justice boys. We're still the No. 1 firm – thanks to you,' Dermot said, brushing down his suit.

I shudder to admit it, and I certainly wouldn't say it out loud, but I actually enjoyed the melee. I knew it was wrong, but something about it felt kind of liberating. I'm not sure what came over me.

We regrouped in a small pub. Dermot ordered drinks for everyone and swallowed another two Nurofen with his Guinness. He must be plagued with headaches.

'Who was that I hit?' I asked him.

'Only the top man in the Department of Justice,' he said. 'Everyone in government will fear the IMF now!'

That hadn't been my intention.

'Tell me,' I said, 'There's something I've been curious about. How did you get to be top man in Finance?'

'Length of service,' he replied, with a knowing grin.

'But you can't be much older than me. How could that be?' I asked.

'Simple,' he said. 'They made a mistake. How else?'

We ordered more drinks. Dermot went to the toilet and I picked up a free newspaper and read a strange story about an Irish disc jockey on a plane with some Nurofen Plus. So that's what they were up to, I thought, as Dermot returned looking pleased with himself.

'I'd better get back to Ajai,' I said. 'What will I tell him? What's your negotiating position? What's your bottom line?'

Dermot looked puzzled. 'Sure give us whatever you can manage,' he said. 'That's all anyone can do. After all, I trust you.'

'What? He trusts us? He TRUSTS us?'

I had never seen Ajai lose control of himself but he was on the verge of it now. It was Sunday morning and we had been up most of the night finalising the Irish bailout, without the Irish. He went into his office and didn't emerge for two hours.

'Everyone negotiates,' he said. 'Why won't he negotiate? What is he playing at? Is he looking for deniability on a deal he didn't negotiate, or is he just an idiot? What should we do? You've spent time with the man, what's your take on this?' Ajai asked me.

'Realistically, we can do anything we want,' I said reluctantly – part of me felt like I should be trying to do Dermot a good turn. 'They'll sign anything we put in front of them.'

'Maybe that's just it,' Ajai thought aloud. 'Maybe they're negotiating by not negotiating. If the deal is too tough, they can renege on it.'

In difficult times in difficult countries I had never seen Ajai lose his composure. Not even for a split second. He may strike fear into the hearts of South American presidents but it was clear to me now that Dermot had him spooked.

I had phoned Dermot that morning and persuaded him to come into the office. He reluctantly agreed because he was meeting people in a pub called Doheny and Nesbitt's. It seemed a bit early for that. Dermot had been in the meeting for just a few minutes when he became agitated and started looking out the window.

'There's no chance this is going to interfere with the rugby is there?' he asked.

Ajai looked at him over his glasses.

'We have been here all night,' he said. 'We will be here all night tonight too. And we need you here,' he said sternly.

'Well, I'm afraid that's not possible,' Dermot said flatly. 'I've already issued a press release cancelling the bailout talks because of the snow.'

Ajai spat coffee across the room.

'What snow?' he spluttered. 'That scattering? Be serious, Mulhearn! You are in bailout talks with the IMF.'

Dermot looked at Ajai with utter disdain.

'Gah,' he said. 'Don't be such a spoilsport. You sound just like Michael Noonan. Were you ever a teacher? You do what you like, Ajai. We're going to make a snowman.'

'When I listen to you, Mr Mulhearn,' Ajai said. 'I find it very hard to believe that Ireland ever had a booming economy. Your country is facing ruin. Do you understand that?'

'Well, I'll have you know that we had a very booming economy,' Dermot replied sniffily. 'We've faced disaster before, you know. When necessary, heroes have died for Ireland. Granted those were different times and those people had very little else to be doing with their time. Still, we are well capable of struggling through. More importantly, Ajai, do you not realise that this is a *Sunday*? Who ever heard of a public servant working on a Sunday? And it's snowing. We always take time off when it snows; it's a public service tradition.' He got up to leave. 'Good day, gentlemen,' he said as he slammed the door behind him.

Ajai sank into his chair. He took off his glasses and rubbed his temples. He looked at me and through me at the same time. 'Go and keep an eye on that idiot,' he said coldly. 'Go to the rugby with him. Go wherever he goes. Don't let him out of your sight and don't let him waste any more money.'

I went, but I worried. I couldn't get into the spirit of things at the rugby. It's not really a game I understand. The newly built Aviva stadium was impressive though. It looked as if all the building in Ireland had been an exercise in showing off. I left Dermot in a pub near the stadium and returned to the office to see where things stood. Ajai was gone but he had left a note on my desk.

'Give this document to Mr Mulhearn for his Taoiseach

to announce,' the note read. 'It is clear to me now that the main condition of any Irish bailout should not be the repayment terms but the degree of oversight we have on Irish budgetary affairs. That is where you come in.

'I am appointing you Dublin Bureau Chief for the IMF. Congratulations, if they are appropriate. I will review your position in twelve months.

'By the way,' the note concluded, 'we decided on a combined interest rate of 5.8 per cent. See that they make the payments.'

I was still staring dumbly at the note when Dermot came into the office two hours later. He was with some Argentine rugby supporters who he was showing around Dublin. 'We're going to Shanahan's,' he said. 'Will you come and join us? I want to show these feckers that our beef is better than theirs.'

'No, thank you,' I muttered weakly.

'Suit yourself,' he said. Then he noticed the piece of paper in my hand. 'What's that? Is that the bailout document? Have you something for the Taoiseach to announce? I'll be seeing him later. We always have a trad session on a Sunday night.'

I gave him the document from Ajai. Dermot folded it in half and put it in his pocket.

'Do you not want to know what's in it?' I asked.

'Whatever for? It won't make a blind bit of difference to me. In any event it will be better coming from the Taoiseach,' he said with a wink. 'The Irish people fought long and hard for the right to be shafted by their own kind.'

'Is that what they fought for?' I asked him. 'I thought I read something about fighting for freedom?'

'Indeed,' said Dermot.

TWO

WE OPERATE IN
THE GREY AREA

☆ ☆ ☆ ☆ ☆ ☆ ☆ ☆ ☆ ☆ ☆ ☆ ☆ ☆ ☆ ☆ ☆ ☆

The next day I was sitting at my new desk in the Department of Finance at seven o'clock in the morning. Whenever I start a new assignment I like to get my feet under the desk early. It creates a good impression and lets everyone know that the IMF is in town and we mean business. I generally find that the people I work with soon follow my lead and start coming into work early too. However, on this occasion I was still alone in the office at 10.30 a.m. There was no sign of anybody from the Department. As I crossed the road to the office, I had seen other people making their way to work, so I knew it wasn't a public holiday.

At least I no longer have to bribe the security guard with €20 every time I want to get into the office. I negotiated with him and we eventually reached agreement. He was a tricky customer but at least he turned up to work. At first I insisted that no one should have to pay to get into their office but he was utterly unimpressed with this argument and he pointed out that jobs in this country were increasingly hard to come by. 'There's plenty of people who would pay for the chance to work,' he said with exasperating logic. So we came to an arrangement whereby I would pay him €20 per week for constant ongoing access to the office. I must admit I was quite pleased with myself, having bargained him down from his initial demand for €50. He refused point blank to issue me with a receipt however. There seems to be a deep-seated mistrust of receipts here.

When I finally got into the office, I was surprised to find that the floor was littered with party hats and streamers. Empty champagne bottles lay scattered around, and, unpleasantly, there was a used condom on my desk, which was right in the middle of the room. I lifted it with a pen and put it and the pen in a bin.

I can only assume that my new colleagues went from celebrating the rugby to celebrating the bailout. They may not know how to negotiate but they certainly know how to enjoy themselves.

Two cleaners came in at 9.30 a.m. but they didn't clean up.

'Look Rose, cham-pay-en,' said one, giving the word 'champagne' a mysterious extra syllable.

'Deadly, Ruby,' said the other. 'I love cham-pay-en.'

'D'ye want some?' Rose asked me to my surprise.

'It's 9.30 in the morning,' I replied, perhaps a little sniffily.

'Oooh, suit yourself,' she said. 'Come on, Ruby.'

With that they were gone, taking the last few bottles of champagne with them and leaving me to tidy the mess. I wouldn't be able to work in it – no reasonable person could. Half an hour later the office was beginning to look fit for purpose, although I had not been able to do anything about the stains on the carpet.

One by one, hungover civil servants started to arrive at around 11 a.m. They huddled in small groups by the photocopier and the watercooler, washing down Nurofen Plus with black coffee. They spoke in muffled tones but stopped talking and looked suspicious whenever I glanced over at them.

At midday Dermot arrived, fresh as an ocean breeze. Somehow his single-minded pursuit of a good time never seemed to result in a hangover. With the obvious exception of unpredictable flashes of anger whenever reality intruded on his day, I had yet to see anything affect his composure for long.

'You're still here,' he said, looking around. 'You have the place looking nice. If I give you some petty cash would you pick up some orchids? They'd set the room off nicely.'

'Ajai seconded me to the Department for twelve months to oversee the adjustments you need to make to ensure that the bailout succeeds,' I said. 'He didn't say anything about orchids.'

'Is that right? I'll have to ask the Minister to get the flowers so. Twelve months, you say? You'll be needing an apartment,' he said. 'I know just the place for you.'

'The hotel will do fine for the moment,' I said, 'but I

will obviously have to economise. The IMF isn't made of money.'

Dermot laughed until he realised I wasn't joking.

'Well you're not alone there are you,' he said, affecting a more serious note. 'I hear economising is the new going out. I don't think it will catch on. How is Ajai by the way? Did he leave cash or a cheque? I hope he left some of it in cash.'

I rubbed my temples. 'He left neither,' I said. 'There is a long road to be travelled before we release any funds.'

'Is there indeed?' said Dermot. He was momentarily vexed, as though he had had immediate plans for the money. 'Will we be passing Leopardstown on our travels, do you think?'

I was trying not to lose my temper.

'Did you have a chance to read the terms and conditions in the Memorandum of Understanding on the bailout?' I asked him.

'The terms and conditions?' he said. 'No one reads them. Come on, I'll buy you lunch.'

Another lunch with Dermot. I could feel the button on my trousers digging into soft flesh. I have always been conscious that a sedentary lifestyle can lead to piling on the pounds. I rarely snack at work and usually have a green salad for lunch. Dermot doesn't believe in green salads. He won't allow anyone eating with him to order anything that might pass as healthy. I couldn't face any more rich food – he already had me so full of foie gras I felt like a fat duck. I told him I was in the middle of slashing his department's spending for the first quarter of 2011 and would have a sandwich at my desk.

'Suit yourself,' he said.

Dermot came back from lunch early. I hadn't been around for long but I knew that meant something was wrong, seriously wrong. I was right. He stormed into the office like we didn't own the place.

'What's all this?' he asked, throwing the morning newspapers on my desk.

'Terms and conditions of the bailout,' I said. 'You did realise there would be terms and conditions, didn't you? I asked you this morning if you had read them.'

'Of course I knew there would be terms and conditions,' he fumed. 'But there's no grey area. This is utterly transparent. We operate in the grey area – without it we can't function properly – and I can't find it.'

'The IMF is not made up of politicians,' I told him. 'We do grey suits, not grey areas. Nor, for that matter, should you.'

'Don't be ridiculous,' Dermot shot back. 'If we don't have a grey area, we'll have a black economy. Do the IMF do black economies?'

I didn't bother to reply as Dermot sank into a chair and opened the Memorandum of Understanding.

'Weekly reports, monthly reports, quarterly reviews,' he

lamented. 'Balance sheets, adherence to targets. It's like a secret language, complete mumbo jumbo.'

Suddenly, as is his habit, Dermot brightened. His capacity to change mood is truly extraordinary.

'I get it. This is just for the optics,' he said, winking at me 'No one actually reads these reports, do they? I bet you have warehouses full of unread reports back in Washington.'

'Ajai reads them,' I said. 'He learns them off by heart. Ajai can recall every minute detail of every report he has ever read. It's very impressive.'

Dermot looked crushed. He reached into his pocket for some Nurofen Plus and dry swallowed quite a few of them.

'I'm going to talk to the Brians. They won't like this one bit,' he said, as though it mattered whether the Brians liked it or not. He left abruptly.

I didn't see Dermot again until I got out of the shower in my hotel bathroom that night and he handed me a towel. I wrapped the towel around my waist.

'I wish you would stop letting yourself into my room,' I said. 'I find it very disconcerting. Couldn't you have phoned from reception?'

'I did, but you were in the shower,' he said with flawless logic.

'What is it you want, Dermot?'

'The Brians aren't happy,' he said gravely. 'Not happy at all. Particularly about this business of us paying some of the bailout ourselves. €17 billion? That's a bit rich, isn't it?'

'But you gave them the document to sign,' I said. 'Surely

they read it? Nothing in it should be a surprise to them.'

'Come off it,' said Dermot. 'They were never going to read the damn thing.'

'Well you should have read it then, or at least attended the negotiations,' I said.

Dermot sat down at the edge of my bed.

'But I have nothing in common with Ajai,' he explained. 'I'm used to negotiating with people I know – people I went to school with or people I play golf with – friends. How on earth am I supposed to negotiate with a perfect stranger? It makes no sense. Our negotiations take place in a framework of social partnership. You get to know each other first. You look after each other. That's how we negotiate round here.'

'How has that worked out for you?' I asked.

'It was grand until you came along,' Dermot said bitterly.

He jumped to his feet then, suddenly smiling broadly.

'Let's forget the bailout. Come on for a drink,' he said. 'Tonight is for celebrating.'

I was beginning to find his sudden shifts of mood dizzying.

'Celebrating?' I said. 'Celebrating what?'

'Don't you follow the news at all? It's not every day that England don't get to host the World Cup. Come on, the Taoiseach will be singing. It'll be great craic. It always is.'

And it was. If the Irish redirected a fraction of the energy that they put into partying towards negotiating, I'm sure they would have got a much better deal from the EU on the bailout. They may even have got to burn the bond-holders, which would have been a real excuse for a party.

We met in a pub called MacIntyre's, just around the corner from my hotel. The Taoiseach was already holding court when we came in and he continued to do so until the early hours of the morning. There was a small group of government ministers and senior civil servants hanging on his every word, but I couldn't help notice that they kept exchanging knowing glances, as though the Taoiseach was the butt of a joke that none of them had bothered to tell him about. He has a great voice for the kind of ballads you would hear in the Irish bars in Jersey, and his voice is strong enough for him to sing unaccompanied. But his real gift is as a mimic. He had spent just a few short minutes in Ajai's company but he had him down. It was impossible not to laugh.

'This is not the first time the IMF has put together a programme in a country that is just about to face an election,' Mr Cowen said. I was pretty sure he was quoting verbatim from an interview Ajai had given the *Financial Times*. 'In fact this happened in Korea in 1997. It happened in Brazil. So we have experience with this. And it's quite striking in such situations that governments are responsible. They do the right thing. They do what needs to be done.' It could have been Ajai saying those words; the mimicry was perfect. But Mr Cowen had a broad, vulgar smirk on his face as he said the last lines about governments doing the right thing. It was clear that neither he nor his audience believed it for a moment.

The Taoiseach was actually a very likeable man when I

met him in person. 'A chara Gael,' he said to me, as he shook my hand warmly before pulling me into an inappropriate bear hug. 'The IMF will always be welcome here.'

Just then a wild blonde woman with bright red lips and a slightly deranged grin dragged me away from the bar to a small dancefloor.

'Come on the Eighty-five Billion Euro Man,' she roared. 'Show us your fucking moves.' She held me in a vice-like grip, spinning me round and round and mouthing the most outrageous expletives in my ear.

'I'm not used to dancing,' I said awkwardly.

'You're right, you're shite,' she said, smiling in an unhinged way as she threw me onto a chair the Minister for Finance had just vacated and went in search of her next victim.

'Who on earth was that?' I asked Dermot after I had caught my breath.

'Do you like her? That's Sweary Mary,' he said. 'She's the government minister in charge of education no less. This is a great little country and no mistake. She's the Tánaiste too, of course.'

'Tánaiste,' I struggled a bit with the Gaelic word. 'What is a Tánaiste? Is it a medical condition?'

'Hah,' said Dermot. 'It might well be! But no, the Tánaiste is the Taoiseach's deputy. If anything should ever happen to Cowen, Mary will be in charge of Ireland and of all the money you're giving us.'

'Lending you,' I corrected.

'Whatever,' said Dermot. I made a mental note to tell

Ajai about Sweary Mary. Then I thought better of it and made a mental note not to tell Ajai anything at all about her.

I went out to get some air and regain my composure and found the Taoiseach sitting on a barrel singing quietly to himself.

'I wish I had someone to love me, I'm weary of being alone,' he sang.

'Very nice, Taoiseach,' I said as he finished the song and lit a cigarette.

'Ah, my American friend,' he said, and then he muttered something. I didn't quite catch it but it sounded like he said 'my only friend'. Anyway, I thought it best to pretend I hadn't heard it.

'That was a lovely song, Taoiseach,' I said.

'Yes,' he said. 'A lovely song, a lovely song.' Suddenly he became slightly belligerent. 'Do you know,' he said, 'that for better or worse I am the captain of this sinking ship, but I have to come out here in the freezing cold to have a smoke because of Micheál bloody Martin and his stupid fucking smoking ban. What do you think of that? Do you think that's right or fair or proper?'

I looked at him and around me. There was no one there to help with what was turning into an awkward situation. 'Micheál bloody Martin?' I asked nervously.

'Yes. Bloody Micheál bloody Martin. Bloody smarmy eejit. Bloody do-gooder. Bloody Minister for Foreign Affairs Martin,' Mr Cowen almost shouted while waving his hands in the air.

'I don't think I've met him,' I said.

'Oh you'd know if you had,' Mr Cowen said. 'He likes to sing and tell jokes too, but he never joins in when I'm singing. He just watches and waits. If he wants my job that badly he should bloody well ask for it.'

Mr Cowen turned around to pick up his drink and I took the opportunity to ask him if he thought the bailout would work and that the Irish economy would recover. 'Of course it will,' he said. 'We are where we are but we'll be where we'll be when we get there. Obviously, we're after going backwards but the brakes have been applied and going backwards has been brought to a halt. We'll be going forward now going forward. It has to be acknowledged that forward is better than backwards. Forward is the future and backwards is the past. Onwards and upwards, eh? Do you know any songs?'

Confused, I left him singing on his own and went back to the party. The Minister for Finance grabbed me as I entered the room. 'I bet you can't guess when I'm spoofing?' he said to me, breathlessly.

He backed me up against a wall and started making wildly contradictory statements. 'You'll never guess,' he said.

It was a strange party trick but there's no denying he was good at it. Neither I nor the people who joined us were able to tell the difference between when he was spoofing and when he was telling the truth. Unfortunately neither was he.

'It's his great gift as a politician,' Dermot told me. 'He has no idea when he is telling the truth and he has no idea that he has no idea when he is telling the truth.'

'I noticed that he sheds a solitary tear every time he mentions the word "Ireland",' I said.

'I taught him that,' Dermot said proudly. 'Great, isn't it? Works wonders on the plain people of Ireland. They lap it up.'

It was only as I walked back to the hotel that I remembered I had promised Dermot I would do the Department of Finance reports for Ajai for him. Oh well. I was pretty sure they wouldn't be done otherwise.

There were extraordinary scenes in the office the following morning. Everyone was in on time, quietly sitting at their desks, glued to their monitors. They appeared to be somberly working away. Could it be that the reality of their country's situation had dawned on them? Had they realised their mistake in not bothering to negotiate and letting the ECB back them into a corner on defaulting? It wasn't too late. I approached Dermot.

'You know,' I said. 'At the first review the IMF would be quite happy to support you if you wanted to default on the banks. That is provided you adhere to our ... I mean your ... budgetary strategy.'

Dermot looked at me blankly.

'How could you? How could you talk about money at a time like this?' he said indignantly, and his eyes returned to the screen.

'What is it?' I asked. 'Has there been some terrible trag-
edy? Has the Government fallen?'

'Government? Your priorities are shot. It's Leslie
Nielsen. He's dead.'

I've always liked Leslie Nielsen but he clearly didn't
mean as much to me as he did to the Irish civil service. As I
went from desk to desk I saw that all the staff were reading
the news of Leslie Nielsen's demise and not working as I had
naively assumed.

Suddenly, Dermot stood to his full height and
addressed his staff in a grave tone I hadn't heard him use
before. 'Leslie Nielsen would not want us to be sad,' he
said. 'He dedicated his life to farce, and we must honour
that.'

'Liam,' he said to one of his assistants, who jumped to
attention, 'phone Mitchell's and get them to deliver champagne without delay. Charge it to our account. It must
be here when I come back from the bathroom. Tom, get
some inflight magazines and Nurofen Plus. Seán, call all
the other departments. Tell them to cancel their meetings
and divert all calls. We're having a wake!'

The Chiefs of Staff of every government department
attended the wake, including David Mulcahy, the head of
the Department of Justice who I had walloped the other
day during the march. He was very good about it I have to
say. He gave me a bear hug and congratulated me warmly
on my appointment. It was revealing to see all the department heads together. They clearly all shared the same
expensive taste in clothes and accessories but there was
also an obvious hierarchy. As the Chiefs of Staff of what

were considered the two most important departments of government, Dermot and Mulcahy were deferred to on all matters by their colleagues.

I had a lot of paperwork to do so I left the senior civil servants to their 'mourning' and got on with my work – making sure that their country could be governed efficiently and effectively on budget. Every now and again I looked up and saw them gathered in small groups, gesticulating wildly and waving inflight magazines in the air. I couldn't see what they were doing but I could hear frenzied shouts.

'Can you fly this plane and land it?' I heard Dermot shout.

'Surely you can't be serious?' someone else in the group replied.

'I am serious ... and don't call me Shirley,' Dermot yelled, causing uproarious laughter among the group.

I'm not sure that I will ever acclimatise to this country.

I went for a quiet drink on my own after work. I needed some respite from the madness and wanted to break the monotony of another night alone in the hotel. I didn't speak to anyone as I nursed my drink but I overheard a conversation about the IMF, the bailout and the European Union. People here really are furious with the Government for squandering the illusion of wealth that they had promoted for so long. Just before I left to go back to the hotel the conversation shifted to discussing the snow that was still falling steadily outside. This presented another opportunity to be angry with the Government. People here, I was beginning to realise, could be angry with the Government over pretty much anything.

Back at the hotel Dermot had left a note inviting me to join him for dinner. I couldn't face it, so I phoned him and explained that I had an important call with Ajai scheduled.

'Booooorrrrriiiiinnngg,' Dermot bellowed down the phone.

'Needs must,' I replied.

I lay in bed and watched *I'm a Celebrity Get Me Out of Here*. It would solve a few problems if I could introduce evictions in the Department of Finance. Then, as I flicked through the channels I came across an Irish version of *The Apprentice*. I hope Ajai never gets to see it. Judging by the contestants, it could be a long time before we get our money back.

On Friday I once again found myself working alone in the Department of Finance. The Budget was due to be delivered on the following Tuesday and there was plenty of work to be done before it was published. Despite this everyone had gone Christmas shopping. It's a tradition, apparently.

'That's our money they're spending,' Ajai said when I told him on Skype.

'I know,' I said, 'but if it's any consolation they probably spend a lot less when they're shopping than they do when they're "working".'

'Did Dermot go shopping too?' Ajai asked.

'Errr.'

'Don't you know where he is? You're supposed to be keeping track of him.'

'I know where he is, Mr Chopra,' I said. 'He went to a rugby match in Wales. He and one of the junior ministers took the government jet.'

'Are you serious?' said Ajai.

'I know. I'm sorry,' I said. 'I couldn't go with him. Somebody has to prepare this damn Budget.'

Ajai hung up.

I worked through the weekend making sure that the Budget would indeed meet its target of frontloading €6 billion of savings for the exchequer. I had to phone Dermot from time to time to clarify some of the items of spending. He came back from the rugby on Saturday morning but he was not happy as Leinster had only managed a draw with Scarlets.

'Isn't a draw away from home a good result?' I asked him.

'Oh, I suppose it is for Leinster,' he said. 'But it's rather dull for me.'

After my third call to him, he told me not to disturb him again.

'I'm having an *X Factor* evening,' he explained. 'This could be Mary's last night. You're welcome to join us.'

I declined his offer and looked again at the Budget submitted by the Department of Education. The information was sketchy at best – it was a one-page document.

Spending was divided into three areas: Staff, Buildings and Stuff. I googled the Department of Education and then I remembered that the Minister was the woman who scared the living daylights out of me at the England-not-getting-the-World-Cup party. I noticed I had started to sweat ever so slightly. I thought about asking her for a more detailed budget submission, then I put my head in my hands and decided I should avoid any further communication with her at all costs. I approved her budget in full without considering whether it had made any savings. If necessary, savings would have to be found elsewhere.

I was just about to leave when Dermot phoned. He was quite emotional.

'Mary's out of the *X Factor*,' he said. 'They shafted her. Bloody Brits. Eight hundred years of oppression and now this! I think we should cancel the Budget as a mark of respect.'

'I don't think Ajai would approve,' I said. 'He's not a big fan of the *X Factor*.'

☆ ☆ ☆

I was surprised to see everyone in the office again when I arrived the next morning. They were all hyped up about the Budget and some of them had gathered around my desk to look admiringly at the document.

'Are you really going to cut ministerial pay?' one of the clerical officers asked. 'You won't get any directorships,' he warned me.

Dermot arrived with the Finance Minister in tow.

'Did you do all this from scratch?' Dermot asked.

'How else would I do it?'

'We usually just take a bit of Tipp-ex to last year's one and change the numbers around a bit, but each to their own.' He turned to face the Minister. 'What do you think, Minister? Is this what the good old days were like?'

'I'd say it is surely,' the Finance Minister replied with great certainty and fervour.

'What good old days?' I asked.

'You know,' Dermot winked at me. 'The good old days. When the British were in charge and we had nothing to do and all day to do it.'

He tapped the heavy document with his index finger and looked me in the eye. 'Is there anything I need to know?' he asked.

'You could always read it,' I said.

Dermot laughed a hollow laugh. 'There's nothing I would rather do,' he said. 'But there simply isn't the time. So spill the beans, why don't you?'

'There are no big surprises,' I said, 'though I did slash your salary.'

'Did you indeed? My wife will be very upset with you.'

'Aren't you?' I asked.

'Not at all. I'm amused. She gets my salary. I live on my expenses.'

I was joking when I said I'd cut his salary, but Dermot was deadly serious.

The next morning was Budget day and the office was

tense with anticipation. We walked to the Dáil with the Minister carrying the Budget document and Dermot's coat. On the way they introduced me to a strange-looking man who shook my hand vigorously but didn't speak English or any language I could understand.

'Who was that?' I asked when he had left.

'That was Jackie Healy-Rae,' Dermot told me, 'a man who will have more influence on this year's Budget than the IMF and the EU combined.'

'I doubt that very much,' I said crossly. I had worked hard on the Budget and was feeling tired and a bit underappreciated.

'We'll see,' said Dermot.

I had to marvel at the way the Minister delivered the Budget as though he wasn't reading it for the first time. It is undoubtedly a talent that he can speak with such authority on subjects he doesn't understand. 'You should have met his father,' Dermot said. 'The apple doesn't fall far from the tree.'

I was so familiar with the Minister's words – after all, I wrote them – that I began to drift off, but I soon came back to my senses when I realised they had dropped a zero on my adjustment to ministerial salaries. Suddenly I was completely alert, conscious that Dermot might have made major changes to the savings in the Budget. In the end he had not adjusted it by much. He had, however, looked after the politicians and the senior civil servants. I made a mental note to be more vigilant.

We went for a few drinks that night to celebrate the

Budget being well received (albeit grudgingly). I left early but Dermot told me the next day that a few of them went to withdraw money from a cash machine and it kept giving them more than they had asked for.

'You should have stayed with us,' he said. 'You could have made a few quid.'

Naturally he was disgusted to hear on the news later that all of the money given out incorrectly by Bank of Ireland cash machines would have to be repaid.

'It's so unfair,' he said. 'They gave us the money! Why should we pay it back?'

'Why indeed?' I said.

A few hours later Dermot came over to my desk shadow boxing, ducking and weaving. 'The gloves are off,' he said, as he made a seamless transition from boxing to karate and performed an elaborate Jackie Chan manouevre on my Greek yoghurt, which splurted all over my desk and my keyboard.

'What are you talking about now, Dermot?' I asked as I rescued some documents from around my desk.

'The Taoiseach put the boot in. There's no one better when he's riled. We're on an election footing.'

'We?' I asked.

'Yes, we,' he said. 'Sure aren't we all in this together?'

It seems that the politicians had a bit of a falling out and the bailout is going to go to a vote in the Dáil next Wednesday. This sort of thing happens wherever we go. We tend to indulge it as it never affects the bottom line. It's important to maintain the appearance of business as usual while people digest the fact that the IMF are now in charge of their finances. At the end of the day, when we come in there's no getting rid of us. Still, as a matter of course Ajai decided to withhold our approval of the bailout until after the Irish politicians had voted. The look on Dermot's face when I told him was priceless.

'You're withholding the money? Are you mad?' he said, aghast.

'You ask for our help then have a vote on whether or not to accept it? Are you mad?' I replied. I was enjoying the conversation.

'But that's just politics,' he said. 'You know what politicians are like. It's not as if they're going to vote against it.'

'I'm sure they won't,' I said. 'But, as you like to say: you're playing senior hurling now.'

I laughed, but Dermot didn't. I think I might have ruined his afternoon.

'Anyway, what are you giving out to me for?' I waved the business section of the newspaper at him. 'You approved those AIB bonuses. When were you planning to tell me about them? Ajai is fuming.'

'Now that's below the belt,' he said. 'Some of those poor unfortunates lost their second homes in the property bubble. The bonuses give them a chance to get back on their feet. That will be good for everyone in the long run.'

'Indeed,' I said, just to annoy him. 'I'm going to get a sandwich.'

When I came back I found the words 'Fuck the IMF I've a horse outside' scrawled on my desk. I had no idea what it meant but I knew that the backlash had begun. Dermot was all over me, promising to find the culprit.

'There will be a full investigation I assure you,' he said.

'Don't bother, Dermot. It's fine,' I said.

I knew it was his handwriting, and he knew I knew. I sent an email to all the staff detailing what the stabling, feed and veterinary costs of keeping a horse amount to. Such luxuries would be beyond the reach of any Irish civil servant in the future, I guaranteed them. That was bound to annoy him.

Of course, the vote on the bailout passed in the Dáil and our executive board approved the billions for Ireland. Unfortunately I had to accept a couple of extravagant arrangements for the support of some independent TDs. Ajai wouldn't like them but that seems to be how business is done here.

Later that very day I caught Dermot and the Finance Minister rifling through my desk. They were utterly brazen.

'The bailout money – where is it?' Dermot demanded when he saw me.

'We itemise all requirements and then you draw it down,' I explained slowly for the hundredth time.

'But it's the weekend,' the Finance Minister said.

'No it isn't. It's Wednesday,' I told him.

'Never mind what day it is,' Dermot said. 'What if we give you Noel Dempsey's seat in Meath? You'd be sure to be elected on the first count. The people love the IMF. You can do no wrong.'

I shook my head. I was never sure when Dermot was joking.

'Why don't I just buy you boys a drink instead?' I suggested.

That seemed to placate them.

I had a few drinks with them and then went back to the hotel to get some sleep. Ajai Skyped me in the middle of the night.

'What the hell is "Jackie the Redeemer"?' he asked.

I groaned inwardly. 'It's a statue of Jackie Healy-Rae,' I explained. 'He's an independent TD in Kerry. He voted with the Government to help pass the bailout package in the Dáil.'

'That idiot? I saw him on the news when I was there. I thought he wanted a hospital,' Ajai said.

'He does, and a university and a statue of himself overlooking the lakes of Killarney modelled on Christ the Redeemer in Rio de Janeiro. If it's any consolation I think he was joking about the university.'

'Never mind the university,' Ajai said. 'Is the statue in Rio gold-plated?'

'No, Ajai, it's not. But it doesn't have a flat cap either. He insisted his cap has to be gold-plated and the statue has to be bigger than Christ the Redeemer.'

Ajai groaned; somewhere in Africa a finance minister suffered a heart attack.

I decided to get all the bad news over with.

'We also had to OK a casino modelled on Sun City to be built in some backwater in Tipperary,' I told him.

'At least casinos generate income,' Ajai said. 'Any good news?'

'Not really, Mr Chopra,' I said. 'Every day there's a new crisis. It was bank bonuses yesterday and whether or not there would be enough grit to deal with the latest snow storm today. I suppose these things keep them occupied while I try to balance their books.'

After about a minute I realised that Ajai had already hung up. I turned over and tried to get back to sleep.

THREE

My Other Home
is a Penthouse

☆ ☆ ☆ ☆ ☆ ☆ ☆ ☆ ☆ ☆ ☆ ☆ ☆ ☆ ☆ ☆ ☆ ☆

I had a sleepless night of tossing and turning in my hotel bed. I had been living in the hotel for too long. Eating rich food with Dermot at work and by myself in the hotel at night was sapping my energy levels. I had put off finding an apartment because I was so busy, but there is only so much 'gracious living' a person can take. The fact that Dermot had constant access to my room didn't really help matters. I felt under siege.

I took to hiding in the bathroom at work as lunchtime approached. I came out once Dermot had gone to yet another of Dublin's fine dining establishments and enjoyed a simple sandwich in Merrion Square. This amused Dermot, who uncovered my ploy when he found me eating alone on a bench in the park and dropped several euro coins into my coffee cup.

I also needed to find an alternative to nights out with drunken politicians and nights in with reality television. Mind you, it was essential that I watched some of these programmes in order to have something to talk about in work with my new colleagues. I can't seem to engage their interest in anything work-related. They forgot all about Mary Byrne as soon as she was voted off the *X Factor*, but this just intensified their fascination with Dr Gillian McKeith.

'Imagine examining poo for a living,' I heard one clerical officer say to another. I took this as the ideal opportunity to try to steer the conversation towards dealing with some of the appalling waste in Irish public expenditure.

'Her job isn't that different from mine and yours,' I said. 'We need to examine expenditure across all government departments to see what's waste and what's worthwhile spending.' The clerical officer rolled his eyes to heaven and stifled a pretend yawn. His colleague stared into the middle distance. 'Blah, blah, blah,' I heard him say under his breath as they walked back to their desks and their respective games of Solitaire. It was as though talking about work might force them to accept that they don't actually do any.

Liam kindly advised me to look up daft.ie for rental properties. He is a helpful and earnest young man who seems utterly lost in the Department of Finance. Dermot ignores him and he is constantly subjected to vicious ridicule by his colleagues. Liam is the kind of young man that the IMF look for when we are on recruitment drives. It is hard to imagine that he has a future in the Department of Finance under Dermot.

I took Liam's advice and had a look on daft.ie while everyone else was on a coffee break. Staff are forbidden to work during that time and couldn't even if they wanted to. All government systems are locked for the duration of the compulsory breaks, with only internet access allowed so that staff can update their Facebook status or watch videos on YouTube.

There certainly appeared to be no shortage of attractive properties on the market but it looked to me as though rental prices still had some downward adjusting to do.

I was looking at what seemed to be a perfectly suitable one bedroom apartment quite near the office when Dermot came running in all out of breath and brought the normal leisurely inactivity that passed for work here to a complete standstill. 'Everyone on the floor! NOW!' he shouted. The entire staff prostrated themselves on the carpet, face down with their arms outstretched towards the entrance. A grim stockily built woman came through the doorway and somehow the temperature seemed to plummet as she moved through the room.

'Get down,' Dermot hissed at me.

'What? Why?'

He sprang up from the floor and dragged me back down to the ground with him before I could protest any further.

The woman tiptoed through the bodies of civil servants, apparently oblivious to them. She gave the appearance of being in another world, as though heavily sedated. She spoke for the first and only time when she reached Dermot. 'Rise,' she said to him.

And rise he did. I went to get up too but felt the woman's shoe on my head. 'Stay where you are,' Dermot whispered.

Dermot reached into his pocket for a set of keys and led the strange woman out of the room.

'Who on earth was that?' I asked as I rose to my feet. 'And what was that about?'

'Don't get up,' said Liam. 'They won't be long. They never are.'

He pulled himself nearer to me on the floor.

'That's Mary Harney,' he whispered, 'the Minister for Health and Children. The Angel of Death. Ice Ice Baby. She has many names. She visits Dermot here and he takes her to the Harney Room. She goes in alone. He waits outside. No one knows what happens in there. Legend has it that there's a solid gold throne in the centre of the room. Dermot has been trying for years to persuade her to become Minister for Finance. It will never happen now though. She used to be the most powerful woman in government. We all feared her but now she's just biding her time till retirement. Only Dermot still believes in her. I think she comes in now just to tease him.'

I made a mental note to monitor Liam more closely. He was the only member of staff I had ever heard make an implied criticism of Dermot. I resolved to speak to Ajai about him. It might be beneficial to have him promoted to a more senior role.

We lay on the floor for some fifteen minutes before they came back and the Health Minister left without a word.

Dermot looked spent.

'She liked you,' I said.

'She did not,' he blushed and looked pleased yet wary that I might be teasing him.

'She did. I could tell,' I said.

'How could you tell?' he asked eagerly.

'Well, there was a little bit of play at the side of one lip, almost like she was about to smile. It was only there when she was looking at you,' I said, leading him on.

'Really? Oh I wouldn't dare believe it,' he said. 'It's such a pity she was never our minister. She's the only one of that lot worthy of the Department.'

'What are you doing anyway?' he asked me as he noticed the web browser open on my computer.

'Looking for an apartment,' I said.

'Didn't I tell you I had an apartment for you?' he said.

'You did, Dermot, but I don't think that would be appropriate.'

'Appropriate indeed,' he said. 'I always thought "appropriate" a very English word. Well, if you change your mind I have just the thing for you,' he said.

Dermot went to a meeting with the Finance Minister then and came back in a dark mood about forty minutes later.

'Your bailout isn't working,' he announced. 'The markets won't buy it.'

'It's not my bailout, Dermot. It's yours. And it would have helped matters if you had stood up to the Europeans instead of rolling over and accepting their first offer. The markets don't believe that you can afford to pay off the European interest. Anyway, even if you can pay it, these things take time to work. The markets need to see that you can make the necessary adjustments, steady the ship and pay the bills. Can you do that?'

'Of course we can,' he said. 'Can't we?'

I looked at him. 'I really don't know,' I said. 'But if you can't you only have yourselves and your greedy ECB buddies to blame. IMF bailouts work. They just take time. There is no magic wand.'

'Oh God, this is a dreary conversation,' Dermot said, looking at his watch.

Liam was standing behind Dermot and I was grateful that he took the opportunity to back me up.

'It is vital to our national interest that we do our best to meet repayments while we renegotiate with Europe,' he said.

I was impressed to see that Liam had a clear grasp of the situation.

'Who asked you?' Dermot said dismissively. 'And what are you doing eavesdropping on our conversation?'

'Sorry, sir,' Liam said. 'I just wanted to inform you that your fitting at Louis Copeland has been cancelled.'

'Well you've done that, haven't you? Now go down to the basement and file something.'

'Yes, sir,' said Liam. 'But sir ... we don't actually have a basement.'

'Then find one,' said Dermot. 'And don't come back until you do.' Dermot turned his back on his junior colleague as he retreated. 'So,' he said to me. 'Have you found an apartment yet?'

'I have a shortlist of two,' I said.

'Great! Get your coat. We'll go for a spin and have a look at them.' Dermot jumped up, he was now full of enthusiasm.

'But your police said on the radio not to make any unnecessary journeys, because of the snow,' I said.

Dermot laughed at me. 'They mean things like work or hospital appointments,' he said. 'This is government business. It doesn't stop for snow unless I want it to. Come on! Show me the ads and I'll phone ahead. It will be fun.'

Dermot took the details I had written down. He raised his eyebrows. 'I didn't think of you as someone who'd want to slum it.'

'What do you mean? Those properties seem perfectly fine,' I said.

'Do they indeed?' he said. He made a few phone calls as we walked to his car. 'All sorted,' he said. 'Hop in.'

'Is this yours? I asked, looking at Dermot's car, open mouthed.

'Yes. Do you like it? We could come to an arrangement if you like. It's nearly two years old now, so I'm due a change.'

I ran my hand along the glistening bonnet of his Bentley Continental GT. 'This,' I said, my throat almost too dry to get the words out. 'This must be €200,000 worth of car.'

'If only,' he said. 'It's almost double that when you allow for our ridiculous Vehicle Registration Tax.'

'I expected you to have something fancy,' I said, 'I thought maybe an S-Class Mercedes … But this …!'

'An S-Class? Good Lord, no! They're as common as

muck. Lenihan has an S-Class. I wouldn't be seen dead in one. Now hop in; it's got a great radio.'

As I settled into the sumptuous leather seat, Dermot played that 'Horse Outside' song that is all the rage at the moment on the handcrafted audio system.

'Aren't The Rubberbandits great?' Dermot grinned. 'We could do with a few lads like them around the office instead of dry shites like Liam.'

'You're very hard on Liam,' I said. 'He seems very responsible and prudent to me.'

'Doesn't he just,' said Dermot with venom. 'Loser!' He made an 'L' sign on his forehead with his fingers.

At the first apartment Dermot took me to, the door was hanging off its hinges and there was what appeared to be human faeces on what might once have been a welcome mat.

'Are you sure this was on the list?' I asked him.

'Oh yes,' he said. 'This is the one "convenient to all things". Except toilets, apparently.'

We got back in the car. I had a feeling Dermot was up to something.

'Where to next?' I asked.

'Let me see,' he said. 'The large ground-floor studio apartment within walking distance of St Stephen's Green.'

We drove for about twenty minutes. Every couple of hundred yards we passed a burnt-out car or a boarded up building. Junkies wandered aimlessly in the middle of the road. Police drove by in squad cars with metal mesh over the windscreens.

'This is taking a long time for somewhere within walking distance of the office,' I said nervously.

'That's just because of the one-way system,' Dermot said. 'You'll walk to work in no time.'

'Or run perhaps,' I said, considering the likelihood of being mugged.

I didn't believe him but there was nothing I could do about it. Somehow that seemed to be always the way with Dermot. Eventually we pulled up outside a derelict building.

'What the fuck are you looking at in your fancy car?' a man on a piebald horse with a plastic bag on his head shouted.

'Do you want to look at this one?' Dermot asked.

'No,' I said. 'Let's go back to the office.'

'As you wish,' he said. 'You know, the apartment I had in mind for you is quite near here. We might as well have a look, don't you think?'

'I suppose so,' I said grudgingly.

Dermot took me to a penthouse apartment in the IFSC with panoramic views of the city and Dublin bay. He drove the car into a parking space beneath a plaque with his name on it and we walked the few yards to the elevator. He used a key in the elevator and it brought us right into the apartment. 'What do you think of your new home?' Dermot asked, gesturing expansively with his arms.

I looked around. It was the ultimate bachelor pad. There was a 52" widescreen TV, a pool table and a fully stocked bar. There were two bedrooms; the master bedroom was ensuite and had a circular waterbed in it.

'It's a bit over the top, isn't it?' I said.

'I don't know what you mean,' Dermot said. 'I think it's very understated – in a Versace kind of way.'

'OK, it's understated, but I can't afford it,' I said, heading for the door.

'Of course you can,' Dermot insisted. 'In fact you should buy it. It would send out a signal that the IMF has faith in the Irish property market. The market has bottomed out, they say.'

'I doubt it,' I said. 'It would be a sign that the IMF has lost its grip on reality.'

'Rent it then' said Dermot. 'I'll look after you. 'You're our guest, after all.' he said.

'How much?' I asked.

'Let me see. Let's call it €3,000 per month.'

'I'll give you €1,000.'

'Let's not squabble over a few euro,' Dermot said. 'I'll meet you halfway, €2,500.'

'That's not halfway.'

'€1,500 then, because you're a friend.'

'OK,' I said. 'But I'll need a receipt.'

'Don't be ridiculous – receipts cost extra.'

I went back into the bedroom and opened the fitted wardrobe. All the gifts of monogrammed clothing that had been in my chauffeur-driven car when I arrived were neatly folded there. I saw the Xbox under the flatscreen TV, and the e-readers lay on the bedside lockers.

'What the hell is going on?' I demanded.

'Oh those things,' he said. 'I just happened to store them here. We couldn't bring them back you see; we never got receipts.'

'I suppose I may as well take them then,' I sighed.

'Oh no, you couldn't possibly,' Dermot said then to my surprise. 'You can't compromise your integrity. No, we'll work out a reasonable price for them. It's the honourable thing to do.'

I was dumbfounded. 'I need to go to the bathroom before we leave,' I said. I sat on the toilet seat staring blankly in front of me and slowly realised that I was looking at the Certificate of Irishness I had been given on my first day in the country. It had been returned with all the other gifts but now hung on the bathroom wall of 'my' apartment. Despite my best intentions I seemed to be always doing what Dermot wanted me to do.

I was in pensive mood as we drove back to the office through the snow. Dermot seemed to know not to push his luck and left me to my thoughts.

The crash, when it happened, came completely out of the blue. Dermot braked suddenly at a green light and we were rearended by the car travelling behind us.

'What the hell happened?' I said. 'Why did you brake?'

'Why indeed?' Dermot replied cheerfully. 'I must be colourblind. Who knew?'

We both got out of the car and walked around to the rear of it. Incredibly, the car that hit us was also a Bentley Continental GT. There couldn't be many of them in Ireland. I was surprised that there were even two. As it turned out, David Mulcahy, Chief of Staff of the Department of Justice had been driving it.

'Ah, the Eighty-five-Billion-Euro Man,' he said warmly. 'How nice to see you again.'

Mulcahy and Dermot nodded at each other and went to survey the damage to their cars, which was minimal: a broken tail light on Dermot's car and fender damage to both vehicles.

'What a shame,' said Dermot cheerfully. 'It's a total write-off.'

'Mine too,' said Mulcahy. 'Terrible pity. How's your back, Dermot? Have you suffered any injury?'

'I fear so,' said Dermot gravely. 'I'm in shocking pain now that you mention it. So is my passenger here, of course,' he added, looking very concerned about my welfare.

They turned to look at me. 'Yes,' said David. 'I can see that. Where would we be without insurance companies, eh?'

'Where indeed?' said Dermot in agreement.

Not for the first time, nor the last, I was totally and utterly speechless.

Back at the office the phones were ringing off the hook but no one was answering them. 'What's going on?' I asked.

'It's just the media,' said Liam. 'We're not allowed to talk to them, you know, like, on the record.'

'Well what do they want?'

'Oh they have a story about a hundred people in the Department getting bonuses,' he said, looking at the floor. I was pleased to see he was shame-faced about it.

'Do a hundred people even work here?' I asked. I had never seen that many.

'Oh yes, and many more,' said Liam. 'A lot of them suffer from back pain though. Some haven't been able to come into work for years and years. It's a poor show to be honest. I wouldn't be surprised if every last one of them was faking it.'

Dermot came swanning in while I was googling the news story about bonuses for the Department of Finance staff who presided over the collapse of the Irish economy. 'Did you get one of these bonuses?' I asked him.

'Of course,' he said.

'What is it for?' I asked.

'For? It's for spending, of course. What else would it be for?'

'No,' I said. 'What did you do to earn it?'

Dermot looked at me, clearly bemused. 'Let me think,' he said. 'Ah, I remember. It was a while ago. We had just approved the AIB bonuses and we decided to give ourselves one too.'

'But you've instructed the AIB to rescind those bonuses,' I said.

'Yes, unfortunate that,' he said. 'Still, onwards and upwards, eh?'

'Well, shouldn't you rescind your bonuses too?' I asked.

'God no,' he said. 'Think how it would look. It would be disastrous. Why it would make us look like the AIB. What possible good would that do? No, like it or not, we're just going to have to accept our bonuses. Take one for the team, eh?'

☆　☆　☆

I checked out of the Merrion Hotel that evening and took a taxi to my new apartment with my few belongings. On my way to work the following morning I stopped in a café for breakfast. A very friendly woman took my order, gave me the newspaper and said she would drop my eggs and toast down to me. She was welcoming, friendly and efficient and I complimented her on her attitude.

'If all Irish people are prepared to work as hard as you, your country won't be in recession for long,' I told her.

'I'm from Prague,' she said.

As I flicked through the newspaper's angry headlines about the economy I could almost hear the indignant talk around the watercooler in the office. One day runs into another at the Department, each full of high drama as one crisis replaces another. There is a storm over bonuses, followed by a storm over removing the bonuses, followed by a storm over reinstating the bonuses, followed by a storm over taxing bonuses. These stories entertained the Department of Finance staff greatly when they were not otherwise engaged in celebrity tittle-tattle or reality TV. On the whole it was more interesting when people were talking about the snow. Ireland isn't used to snow and isn't good at planning for it either. As we faced into a second week of a winter wonderland in Dublin, I found a clearly agitated Mr Lenihan pacing up and down outside Dermot's office with his fingers crossed.

'Is there something I can help you with, Minister?' I asked him.

'You could pray,' he said, 'and cross your fingers too.

It's our only hope, otherwise we might run out of grit and the whole country will come to a standstill because of this bloody snow.'

'But I read only this morning that a new shipment was arriving tomorrow. There should be nothing to worry about,' I reassured him.

'Yes, well, Dermot cancelled that shipment. You see I let the Minister for the Environment order it without first getting Dermot's approval. He's really very annoyed. It's my fault, my fault entirely.'

There really had been quite a bit of snow and I was surprised to see that most of the staff had made it in. I find it amazing that they would go to such lengths to get to work in appalling conditions and then do absolutely nothing when they get there.

'You made it in, you hardy buck,' one would say to another.

'Car spun three times but I didn't want to miss work.'

'Good man yourself. What will we do now?'

'Well, frankly I'm up to my eyes. I'm having a terrible time booking our annual ski holiday for the Easter break. All the best hotels are gone.'

'Why risk coming out in this weather?' I asked one of them. 'Why not work from home?'

They stifled laughter and looked at me with pity. 'As though you'd get anything done at home, what with the tele and everything,' I was told without a hint of irony.

The next drama was all to do with Anglo Irish Bank. I thought perhaps Dermot would be pleased to see that there was finally a prospect that some of the bankers who destroyed the country might face charges. I couldn't have been more wrong.

'This is outrageous,' he said. 'Outrageous!'

'What is it, Dermot?' I asked.

'Files from Anglo have been sent to the Director of Public Prosecutions,' he said, almost in tears. 'These are shameful times. Last Christmas we exchanged gifts with these good people; this Christmas we are having them arrested. I'm too upset to work,' he said. 'Will you come shopping with me?'

Ajai did tell me not to let Dermot out of my sight, but even I was surprised to find myself in a beautician's with him half an hour later. We had looked at Tag Heuer and Rolex watches in Weir's on Grafton Street but Dermot said his heart wasn't in it.

'We'll go and top up our tans,' he said. 'You're looking quite peaky. Come on. The world looks better when you have a tan, don't you think?' Dermot said. 'Poor Seanie FitzPatrick has a lovely tan. I hope it's a comfort to him in these difficult times.'

So the rest of my day was spent listening to Dermot variously sigh and scream as he first had a massage, then what he referred to as a 'back, sack and crack', and finally a sunbed session. Dermot was peeved that I didn't indulge in any of the sessions but I wasn't prepared to spend half my rent in the space of ninety minutes.

The following morning, a Saturday, I was reading the newspaper in a café near my apartment when my mobile rang. It was Dermot.

'You're handy, aren't you?' he said.

'What do you mean by "handy"?' I asked.

'Ah, you know, if something was broken around the house you'd have a go at fixing it.'

'I guess,' I said. 'As long as it wasn't anything major. I'd certainly try not to incur a call out charge.'

'Good man,' he said. 'I'll pick you up in twenty minutes.'

We must have driven for about two hours in heavy snow. Visibility was poor but I knew we were no longer in Dublin. We were driving through hills on a dual carriageway. I was puzzled by a sign that had originally read *Welcome to Wicklow, the Garden County*. Someone had sprayed a black line through the word garden and written the word garbage instead. Dermot smirked when he saw it. 'The whole county is full of illegal rubbish dumps. I suppose it has to go somewhere,' he explained as he threw an empty coffee cup out the window.

Eventually we pulled onto a side road that twisted and turned ever upward. The snow was heavy here and the car sometimes skidded but Dermot seemed entirely oblivious as he turned once again at a sign that said *Kilgrange Boutique Hotel – 1 kilometre*. What was Dermot up to now, I wondered.

We drove along a tree-lined driveway and parked directly in front of the three-storey hotel. It seemed to be completely deserted and reminded me, in the heavy snow, of the hotel in *The Shining*. It was an impressively tasteless building with pretend-Palladian pillars on either side of the neo-Georgian entrance, and a series of Victorian-style bay windows facing the road in all their pebble-dashed glory. The look was completed by a gigantic Edwardian-esque conservatory tacked onto the side of the building. The architecture was nothing if not eclectic.

There were no cars in the carpark and the doors were locked with heavy chains. To my surprise Dermot produced a large bunch of keys and began testing them on the lock on the front door. Moments later we were in the main dining hall of the hotel. Although not huge, the room was very grand with rich oak parquet and a fine marble fireplace. A chandelier that was far too big for the room hung from the ceiling. I guessed you could have seated about sixty there, but it looked as though it was a long time since anyone had eaten in the room. Dermot fiddled with fuses and switches for a while and eventually the light from the dust-covered chandelier revealed the dining room to be full of some kind of machinery.

'Where are we Dermot? Why are we here and why are those machines here?' I asked him.

'This is my hotel. Do you like it? I modelled it on a country house I saw in a magazine at the hairdressers, but I added a few unique touches of my own,' he said proudly. 'Then all the tax incentives ended, so I never opened it. Instead I use it to store these things for the Government. There's good money in it – much better than trying to run the place as a hotel.'

'What are those things?' I asked, pointing to the machines.

'They're electronic voting machines. The best of the best. Top of the range. Sophisticated. Fraud proof. Foolproof. It's a testament to the quality and modernity of our democracy that we have these cutting-edge machines for counting votes,' he said patriotically.

'So what are they doing here?' I asked, perhaps naively.

'Oh we don't use them,' he said. 'Never have, never will. We gave them a trial run a few years ago but they proved far too efficient. Poor Nora Owen lost her seat in ten seconds flat. She didn't even have time to put a face on. Great looking machines though, aren't they? Fierce modern.'

'Wait, Dermot,' I said, 'I don't understand. These must have cost a fortune. Why on earth wouldn't you use them?'

'Oh they did cost a fortune, about €50 million if I remember correctly. Then there's the cost of storing them. There are 7,000 in total. I don't have all of them, mind. I have roughly half of them stored around the country in different hotels and shopping centres. I get about €300,000 a year for hanging on to them. So you're right, there's nothing cheap about them. They're the best of the best, a credit to the nation.'

'Why aren't they used, Dermot?' I asked again.

'Democracy is a very fragile thing, you know. Counting votes needs the human touch,' he told me.

'So why don't you get rid of them then?' I asked him. I was completely perplexed.

'Get rid of them? Why would we do that? They're practically new. No, we have to store them and keep them in pristine condition, which is why we're here today. We need to check the pipes for leaks. I don't want this place flooding when the thaw comes.'

'Well, why didn't you just send a plumber out?' I asked.

Dermot looked at me with pity in his eyes. 'A plumber?' he said, incredulous. 'Sure they're cowboys the lot of them. And anyway, they've all emigrated.'

It took about an hour to confirm that everything was in order and then we got back in the car and began the long drive home. It was a silent journey. Dermot didn't speak to me after I asked him if it had ever occurred to him that it would be easier to just do things right in the first place.

We were finally in sight of the apartment building when his phone rang. I looked at the phone in its handsfree cradle and saw the words 'Biffo calling' light up on the screen.

'Taoiseach,' said Dermot. 'What can I do for you?'

'Good man, Dermot. I want you to pick myself and Lenihan up in ... where are we Brian? ... in the Brazen Head, and take us to Clara. They've been force feeding a bull spuds and it's rat arsed. We're going down to have the craic.'

I had read about drunken bulls in the newspaper that morning. Farmers were feeding them potatoes and they were turning into moonshine – or poitín as they call it here – in their stomachs.

'I can walk from here,' I said to Dermot, but he had already executed a U-turn and we were leaving my apartment behind.

The Taoiseach was in the best humour I had seen him in.

'You're going to love drunk bull baiting,' he said. 'I am proud to introduce you to this ancient tradition.'

'Is it really an ancient tradition?' I asked.

'Absolutely,' said the Finance Minister. 'Wasn't it practiced by Fionn MacCumhaill himself on the slopes of Ben Bulben?'

'No,' said the Taoiseach. 'We made it up this morning.'

The gathering in a field in Clara was a Who's Who of the Government and the civil service. All the Chiefs of Staff were there. The Minister for Education, who I had narrowly survived dancing with a few nights previously, was making lewd gestures at the bull. The Minister for Health stood staring grimly at the bull as though daring it to spill her drink. The Finance Minister was chatting animatedly to a figure in a corner of the field that everyone else knew was a scarecrow. Someone had given the Taoiseach a banjo, and, to the delight of the crowd, he was taunting the tortured animal by playing 'Dueling Banjos' from the movie *Deliverance*. Between him and Mary Coughlan, the bull was being driven demented. It made a charge for Coughlan and she just avoided a goring by scrambling over a fence. The bull turned sharply and crashed to the ground. It was clearly extremely drunk. The Taoiseach strolled over, put his foot on the bull's head and played the last chords of the tune. As he reached the finale, he turned to face the crowd and the bull reared its head and knocked the Taoiseach to the ground. He was about to

trample on Mr Cowen when I managed to divert him with a
blow to the side of the head with a bottle of Jameson.

'Don't waste the good whiskey,' I heard Mary Coughlan
call out. It was the last thing I heard. I turned to run but it
was too late. The bull caught me in the buttocks and threw
me high in the air.

The next thing I remember I was blinking in the bright
lights of a hospital accident and emergency ward. I was lying
face down on a trolley, wearing only a hospital gown, with
the Taoiseach and the Minister for Finance sitting on the
trolley beside me and taking it in turns to apply pressure to
my wounded rear. The Taoiseach sang quietly to himself,
seemingly oblivious to his surroundings. Dermot was sitting across from us in a comfortable armchair with a pretty
nurse on his knee asking him if he was OK. We were also
surrounded by police officers and I wondered for a moment
if we were under arrest, but Dermot explained that he had
called them to protect the Taoiseach and Minister from the
doctors and nurses. Initially I was surprised at this, much to
Dermot's amusement.

'Surely no doctor or nurse would hurt anyone deliberately, never mind the leader of the Government,' I said.

'Are you joking? These people work twenty-hour days in
appalling conditions only to have their wages cut. No one in
their right mind would stand for it,' said Dermot. 'If I were
you I would take a scalpel to the fecker' he said cheerfully to
the nurse on his knee.

Eventually a nurse came to see us, but after a cur-
sory examinination she informed us that we weren't drunk

enough to be treated. The Taoiseach argued belligerently but she got us to walk a straight line and proved her point. So we had to send the Minister for Finance out with some of the police officers for a few bottles of whiskey. Nearly two bottles later, the nurse checked us again. When she saw that I had vomited and the two Brians were headbutting each other, she finally agreed to have my wound stitched and dressed.

The sun was rising when we finally left the hospital. Dermot, still inebriated, dropped me home. I invited him and the Brians in but they said they were off to an early house before they lost their buzz. I spent the rest of the weekend face down on the bed trying not to scratch the thirty-seven stitches in my ass.

~FOUR~

DERMOT GETS NAMA'D

✿ ✿

My flight home for Christmas was cancelled because of the snow at Dublin Airport and they couldn't get me on a flight until 27 December. I had been looking forward to enjoying some low-fat American food for a change, but the reality is that there is always a tension in the house when I go home for Christmas. My father and three brothers enjoy a 'traditional' Irish Christmas: they start drinking as soon as they get out of bed. I'm the black sheep of the family. They are all firemen and their idea of fun is far removed from mine. As for my ex-fiancee, Lisa, I haven't spoken to her since I walked in on her and my brother Tom in a compromising position.

Still, the thought of Christmas alone in Dublin didn't exactly fill me full of cheer either. Dermot must have noticed that I was not myself.

'What's wrong with you?' he asked. 'Anyone would think it was your money we're spending.'

I smiled weakly. 'My flight home for Christmas has been cancelled,' I explained. 'I'm at a bit of a loose end.'

'Sure what of it?' he said. You can spend Christmas with us. Sinéad is dying to meet you. She loves a man with money. And the twins have been pestering me about meeting the man from the IMF.'

'I doubt that, Dermot,' I said.

'You shouldn't,' he said, and he mimicked his children. 'You're, loike, totally famous.'

I was taken aback by Dermot's kindness. 'I'd hate to intrude,' I said.

'Don't be ridiculous,' he said. 'Sure, it would be nice to have someone to talk to for a change.'

'Well, if you're sure your wife won't mind ...' I said.

'Mind? Why would she mind? It's all settled. I'll pick you up on Christmas morning. Now let's go and get some lunch.'

I looked at my watch. It was 10.45 a.m.

'Isn't it a bit early, Dermot, even for you?'

Dermot laughed. 'We're going to swing by the hospital first. A cousin of mine is a surgeon. He'll take a look at our injuries from the crash the other day.'

'What injuries? I don't have any injuries. You don't have any injuries, do you?'

'Look at you bent over your desk like Quasimodo. We have to get you seen to,' Dermot said. 'Didn't you tell me yourself that you had a pain in the neck.'

'That was with you when I was trying to figure out why you fund private hospitals through the public health service. I still have a pain in the neck with it. It makes no sense.'

'You see,' said Dermot. 'The pain you are suffering is making you cranky. If we don't get it treated you could end up suffering from depression, and God knows there's enough depression in this country. So get your coat. As to the private hospitals, they take care of the sick. It would have been sinful not to help them. Sinful.'

The waiting room was crowded with pale, gaunt, chronic-pain sufferers. Dermot breezed past them and told me to follow him. I felt uncomfortable skipping past people who were clearly genuinely suffering but I was with Dermot and he seemed to know where he was going. We found ourselves in a room with a small dapper man in his forties, dressed in a beautifully tailored three-piece suit, playing Solitaire on his computer. He initially looked iritated at the intrusion but just as he was about to rebuke us he recognised Dermot. He rose from his chair, came around his desk and shook Dermot's hand warmly.

'Ah, Dermot,' he said, 'how have you been? I haven't seen you in an age. When was the last time we had dinner? We must be long overdue. Let's arrange something before you leave. My treat.'

'That's very kind of you, Lorcan,' said Dermot. 'I can't think when the last time was. I don't remember seeing you since we played golf in Sandy Lane last year.'

'Ah yes, Sandy Lane,' said Lorcan. 'That was a marvellous few days. And Seanie paid for everything. He wouldn't let us put our hands in our pockets. Those were the days, eh? We were all developers then.' Suddenly the surgeon's good humour left him and he shook his head sadly. 'Poor Seanie,' he said. 'We won't be going to Sandy Lane with him again any time soon. The bloody media have ruined this country.'

'It's a shame,' agreed Dermot. 'Those days are gone for Seanie. But we should get our secretaries to try and book something just for us. Mustn't let standards slip!'

'Great idea, Dermot. Get your girl to call my girl and sort something out. Now what can I do for you? You haven't had another accident, have you?' said Lorcan with a wink.

'"Fraid so,' said Dermot. 'I'll need the usual report. And I want you to look after this man. Give him the works, whatever he needs. He's a guest of the nation.' Dermot turned to me. 'You're in good hands with Lorcan,' he said. 'I have to go and get something done about these terrible crows' feet. The strain you IMF people have me under is aging me dreadfully. I'll pick you up at twelve and we'll go for lunch.'

Before I could object he was gone.

'Now,' said Lorcan. 'Let's have a look. Where's the pain? Describe it for me.'

'There is no pain,' I said. He looked very worried by this, as though he feared my condition might be terminal.

'Tell me what happened,' he said.

'We were in a minor traffic accident,' I said, beginning to lose patience with the situation. 'We were rearended. But no one was hurt. I'm fine.'

'I see,' said Lorcan. 'Turn around and let me have a look.'

I felt his hand on my neck and then the pressure of his thumb between two vertebrae. Suddenly I felt a sharp pain there and a shooting, stabbing sensation down my right arm. I let out a yelp. 'No pain, eh?' he said, shaking his head. 'This is very common. You think you have no pain but you are in fact in agony. Let's have a look at the scan.'

This confused me for the simple reason that I hadn't had a scan.

'See these roundy bits,' he said pointing at someone's vertebrae on a scan, which, bizarrely, he held up to the light coming through his office window. 'I'm going to have to remove them,' he said seriously. 'I'll try to fit you in today, seeing as you're a friend of Dermot's and the pain is so acute.'

I quickly came to my senses. 'That's not my scan,' I said. 'I haven't had a scan done.'

At this, Lorcan became defensive.

'That's hardly my fault,' he said huffily. 'There's been cutbacks since you lot came to town. Anyway, one scan looks much the same as the next. I've seen it all before.'

'I don't want any of my vertebrae removed,' I said, my voice rising.

'Your what?' Lorcan asked.

'My vertebrae. The roundy things.'

'Suit yourself,' he said, 'but you have far too many for a man of your height.'

'I'm not having surgery, thank you very much.' I reached for my jacket but had trouble putting it on. I had severe spasms of pain running from my neck down my right arm.

'Relax,' said Lorcan. 'Perhaps you're right. Most back pain is related to depression anyway.'

I looked doubtful.

'Are you working in a stressful environment? Of course you are. You have to save Ireland from Dermot! That can't be easy!' he said and laughed at his own joke. 'I'll give you a prescription for some anti-depressants, anti-inflammatories and muscle relaxants and we'll see how you get on. I find you get the best effect if you take them with a couple of glasses of wine.'

I took the prescription just to get out of there. Dermot was waiting for me in the ambulance bay at the entrance. When I got into the car I noticed that his crows' feet had completely disappeared and the area around his eyes was eerily expressionless.

'What did you get?' Dermot asked as we drove off.

'Prozac, Difene and Valium,' I told him.

'Goody! I hear they go great with red wine,' he said.

'Who was that crazy man?' I asked. 'What is he actually qualified to do?'

Dermot was indignant. 'That "crazy" man is captain of Royal County Dublin and plays off scratch. He's on so many State Boards I can't keep track. Lorcan couldn't be more highly qualified to do whatever he pleases.'

'Is he qualified as a surgeon, Dermot?' I pressed him.

'I have absolutely no idea,' said Dermot. 'Come on, we'll get your prescription filled. You look to be in a bad way and I want to try that Difene stuff.'

We got back to the office later that afternoon just in time to do Kris Kindle. My recollection of it is slightly hazy as I had had no choice but to take some Valium to relax the muscles in my neck and some Difene for the pain. I didn't take the Prozac.

The Finance Minister was put in charge of proceedings.

Dermot insisted it was good for his morale to give him simple tasks that could be easily accomplished. Mr Lenihan did
seem to enjoy the whole affair and was delighted when it was
his turn to open a present. He received the deeds to a house
on a ghost estate in Mullingar.

'Fantastic,' he said enthusiastically. 'I shall go there on
my holidays.'

I was pleased to see that they had stuck to the €10 price
limit I had imposed. It would be nice to think it boded well
for how the Department would manage the wider economy,
although, in my limited experience, the staff were much better at managing their own finances than those of the nation.

I had bought Dermot an abacus. I thought it would be
a useful aid in introducing him to the principles of macro
economics. I think he knew it was from me.

Dermot was too excited to maintain the anonymity that
is usual for Kris Kindle. With the boundless enthusiasm
of a child with ADHD, he grabbed my present from the
Minister's hands and gave it to me. 'I think you'll be particularly pleased with this,' he said, grinning from ear to ear.

With considerable foresight, Dermot had bought me
a soft cervical collar. Through the haze of medication, I
vaguely remember putting it on.

I normally worked for several hours in the evening when
not out keeping an eye on Dermot, but, as I was drugged
up to the eyeballs, work was out of the question that evening. Instead I watched a *Prime Time Special* on NAMA, one
of the Irish government's bank rescue initiatives set up to
absorb all of the banks' bad loans to property developers.

Apparently every property developer worthy of the name had transferred his assets to his wife before going into NAMA. Indeed, for the wife of a property developer NAMA had resulted in a windfall akin to winning the New York State Lottery, with the added bonus of not having to pay taxes on your jackpot. After a while I flicked over to a light entertainment program called *The Idiot Awards*. It was broadly similar to the NAMA program, minus the vast amounts of cash. On the whole I think it's a good thing that Ajai didn't watch television while he was here.

I spent the next morning in court with Dermot and the Minister, trying once again to sort out AIB. Dermot had persuaded the Minister that there was a need for a Credit Institutions Bill which would give him (Dermot, not the Minister) unprecedented power over the banks.

The Four Courts are very impressive buildings. Dermot told me some of the history of them while we were waiting around. Apparently there was a time when the Irish people were patriotic about more than their banks. This was hard to imagine from my dealings with officials and politicians in the Department of Finance.

Despite a couple of journalists insisting that the public had a 'right to know', the courts saw in Dermot's favour and the department was allowed to essentially take control of AIB without any unwelcome publicity. Dermot spent the rest of the afternoon with his feet on his desk shouting

'Who's your daddy?' down the phone to bankers he had called at random to taunt.

I had never seen him so pleased with himself. 'There's nothing I like more than nationalising banks. I should have thought of it years ago,' he said to me. 'All I want for Christmas is the AIB, the AIB, the AIB,' he sang happily. 'Would you like a bank? I've any amount of them.'

'What's yours is mine,' I pointed out as delicately as I could but he didn't let it dampen his mood.

The Minister for Finance, however, did not share Dermot's good humour. He was clearly distressed and was muttering darkly to himself when I bumped into him in the bathroom.

'I have nowhere to put the AIB,' he said. 'I have no room anywhere.'

'It's OK, Minister,' I said as soothingly as possible. 'Just because the State takes ownership of a bank doesn't mean you have to store it in the Department of Finance.'

'Really?' he said. 'Are you sure? That is a huge relief. Thank you so much.'

Mr Lenihan really is the strangest of men. An hour later I saw him on the *One O'Clock News* claiming that because of his actions AIB would become indestructible. You could see that the interviewer was having trouble keeping a straight face. It was probably all he could do not to ask whether AIB would still be vulnerable to kryptonite. I knew I wouldn't be able to tell Ajai that the Minister for Finance now believed that the Irish banking system was indestructible. I just hoped the international media didn't pick up on it.

I struggled to get into the office the following morning, and not just because I was bent in half with neck and back pain. The hallway was packed with bankers bearing gifts for Dermot. One by one they were granted an audience with him while the Minister for Finance took their coats and brought them drinks. They ignored Mr Lenihan as they sought to secure their futures by making a good impression on Dermot. Before leaving they each dropped to their knees and kissed the ring on his finger.

The gifts began arriving as soon as President McAleese had signed the Credit Institutions Bill into law. One bank even sent a Michelin-starred celebrity chef to cook a special dish for Dermot. Apparently the celebrity chef was almost as notorious as the bankers who sent him. 'His restaurants close almost as soon as he opens them,' Liam explained. 'He's a great chef but he can't run a business.'

To great excitement and considerable confusion, the chef announced that he was going to prepare an ortolan for Dermot's delectation.

'What's an ortolan?' the Minister for Finance asked and the chef fixed him with a withering stare.

'An ortolan,' he said, addressing Dermot and not the Minister, 'is the ultimate culinary delight. It is illegal in several countries but is happily still available to the elite of Ireland.' He spoke with a dramatic flourish as though addressing a royal court.

'Get to the point,' said Dermot. 'What is a bloody ortolan?'

The chef cleared his throat.

'An ortolan is a beautiful songbird,' he said. 'It is tiny and delightful, but the only way to prepare it is by torturing it in the most cruel way imaginable. Some consider it a sin against God and humanity.'

'Sounds great,' said Dermot. 'Let's get started. I'm half starved.'

Excitement spread through Government Buildings as the word went round that one of the most frowned upon acts of the culinary arts was about to be performed on the premises. Within minutes the entire Cabinet was in the office. They were very taken with the celebrity chef in his brilliant whites. The Minister for Finance even ran his fingers through his truffle-oiled tresses in wonder, before being firmly led away by an aide.

As he prepared to roast the beautiful bunting, the chef explained how he had first captured it alive before poking out its tiny eyes. The pitiful creature was then force fed until it was four times its natural size. Before our very eyes the chef then drowned the helpless bird in Armagnac. Then he plucked it and roasted it. I couldn't help noticing that the Minister for Education and Skills, Mary Coughlan, was transfixed by the whole procedure as she dug her fingers deep into the flesh of my arm. 'I fucking love ortolans,' she whispered breathily, 'whatever the fuck they are.'

The chef placed a large napkin over Dermot's head. 'This will help you to savour the aroma,' he said, 'and also to hide your shame at what you are about to do. Now put the ortolan in your mouth with only its beak sticking out, and bite.'

Dermot did as he was told and the beak fell to the floor at his feet.

'As you chew the ortolan,' the chef explained, 'you will feel its delicate bones cutting your gums. This allows you to savour the absolute decadence of what you have done to this beautiful bird. You are enjoying the same meal that President Mitterrand of France ate on his deathbed.'

Dermot was all about the decadence. His own blood and the blood and guts of the ortolan dribbled down his strong chin. 'It wasn't the ortolan that killed him, was it?' Dermot joked. 'Seriously, have you any more of them?'

'I have two more,' the chef said.

'Good stuff,' said Dermot. 'I'll have one and my friend here from the IMF will have the other.' A murmur of discontent went around the room. 'What's wrong with you lot?' Dermot asked the collected Ministers and the Taoiseach. 'Have ye no work to do?'

'We want ortolans,' they said in chorus.

'There's none left. Did you not hear the man?' Dermot attempted to stare them down. For a shocking moment it seemed as though they might actually rebel against Dermot's authority.

At that moment Mary Coughlan intervened. 'Somebody get some fucking sparrows,' she shouted. 'Now!'

Dermot Ahern and Noel Dempsey quickly jumped to the task and the poor bewildered Michelin-starred chef spent the rest of the day roasting sparrows, seagulls and a swan from the pond in St Stephen's Green.

I didn't want an ortolan and instead offered mine to

Ms Coughlan, but she sensed my discomfort and insisted that I 'eat the bollicking bird' in front of her.

I couldn't bring myself to do it. 'I'm sorry,' I said. ' I simply can't. I would be sick. It would be wasted on me.'

'Well we can't have that, can we?' Ms Coughlan said. 'We're in a recession, after all.'

With that she snatched the ortolan from my plate and ate it beak and all.

'What did you do to your neck?' she asked as she crunched on the little animal's bones.

'A car crash,' I explained awkwardly, 'with Dermot. I didn't think I was injured at all but Dermot brought me to see a doctor and for some reason I've been in pain since then.'

She laughed as she pulled a tiny bone from between her teeth. 'Well, you fit right in here, don't you?' she said.

'What do you mean?' I asked her.

'What the fuck do you think I mean?' she asked. 'It's nothing to be ashamed of. I'd say you'll make a tidy packet out of it. Of course you'll have to take prolonged sick leave.'

'Prolonged sick leave? The IMF doesn't do sick leave,' I told her.

'Mean bastards. Sure you're more Irish than IMF at this stage,' she said.

I went and sat down at my desk and examined my conscience. Had I lost my way? Had I been compromised? Was I, as the Education Minister said, more Irish than IMF? Perhaps I should ask Ajai to remove me from the assignment. I considered the facts: On the plus side it seemed that the government was willing to impose severe austerity measures on its people. And the public seemed willing to take the punishment. All the evidence pointed to a genuine willingness among the Irish people to come to terms with the country's problems. On the negative side it appeared that the people who ran the country had learned nothing from experience and were hell-bent on blaming everyone but themselves for the mess their country was in. I didn't hold out much hope of that situation changing. But it didn't have to change. As long as the ruling classes of any country we dealt with enforced austerity measures, it didn't really matter that they themselves continued living the high life.

I had to continue to work with Dermot to make sure the necessary adjustments were made. Spending so much time with him was taking its toll but it was all part of the job. I reassured myself that I was putting the IMF first.

Before I left work that evening, Dermot reminded me that he would pick me up on Christmas morning and take me to his house for dinner.

'Thank you, Dermot,' I said, 'but no more ortolans please. I really couldn't go through seeing that again.'

'Sure an ortolan wouldn't fill a hole in your tooth,' he replied. 'There's no eating in them at all.'

I spent most of Christmas Eve becoming increasingly frustrated with the pain in my neck. Every time I tried to read a report my chin sank down towards my collar bone. I still felt that the surgeon had caused the problem, as bizarre as that sounds, but Dermot insisted that it was typical of soft tissue injuries to flare up a few days after the actual incident.

'How do you know so much about neck injuries?' I asked him.

'Oh, I must have had ten or twelve of them,' he said. 'None as bad as yours though.'

I finally gave in and took two Valium and went Christmas shopping. I bought small, sensible gifts of some placemats for Dermot's wife and selection boxes for his children. Naturally, I kept the receipts.

That night I phoned Dad and my brothers to wish them a happy Christmas, but I got the answering machine.

I had a terrible night's sleep with my neck and spent most of the night pacing around the apartment. I finally fell asleep at around six in the morning and was still out for the count when the doorbell rang at 11 a.m.

'You look awful,' Dermot said when I opened the door.

'Bad night's sleep,' I said. 'Give me ten minutes to shower. Would you like a coffee? I won't be long.'

'No rush,' said Dermot. 'We're not going anywhere. There's been a change of plan.'

Only then did I notice that Dermot was carrying a large turkey in a clear plastic bag in one hand and a toothbrush in the other.

'A change of plan?' I knew this wasn't going to be good.

'The bitch threw me out,' he said. 'I'm staying with you for Christmas. I hope you can cook.'

'What? Dermot, that's terrible. What happened?'

'I came out of the sauna in our en suite and my towel was gone,' he said as he sank into a chair. 'I couldn't find it anywhere. In fact everything that said "His" on it was gone. I had to wrap myself in a towel that said "Hers". My suits were gone. I called Sinéad but there was no answer. I went out the front door to look for her and the wagon slammed the feckin' door behind me. All of my stuff was lying in a pile on the drive. I found my keys in my coat pocket and tried to get back in but she had changed the locks.'

'That's extraordinary Dermot. But something must have happened to cause it? Did you have an argument?' I asked.

'There was no argument. It was a straightforward coup,' Dermot said bitterly. 'I should never have told her that I had signed over the house to her. I knew it would cause problems.'

'What?'

'Oh, she watched that damn *Prime Time* program on NAMA and the next thing you know she asks if I had to sign our properties over to her. I should have known better than to tell the truth. I really should have known,' he said, shaking his head.

'Why on earth would you have signed over your properties to your wife?' I asked, although I wasn't sure I wanted to hear the explanation.

'Sure I had to when we were going into NAMA.' Dermot looked at me like I was a simpleton.

'You're in NAMA?' I sank into a chair across from him.

'Of course,' he said as though I had asked him if the sky was blue. 'You're nobody if you're not in NAMA.'

I put my head in my hands. What would Ajai say to this?

'Anyway, NAMA's not the problem,' Dermot said, 'Sinéad is. She has the house, the holiday homes, the yacht and the two hotels. She has all the apartments, including this one. She's your landlady now. I wouldn't like to be in your shoes.'

'What do you mean?' I asked.

'I'd say the rent will be going up,' he said. 'Anyway, enough of her. You'd better put the oven on or this bird will never be cooked.'

'Where did that come from?' I asked weakly.

'From the kitchen, of course. The window was open. I couldn't climb in without damaging my suit but I managed to pull the turkey through it.'

'You took your family's Christmas dinner?'

'Too right I did,' said Dermot. 'She's robbed me of everything; she wasn't getting the turkey too. That reminds me. You wouldn't pop down to the lobby and pay the taxi driver, would you? She took my wallet.'

After handing over €50 to the taxi driver, I left Dermot to his own devices while I went for a shower. He had asked me if he could stay for a few days until he sorted himself out. Stupidly I told him to make himself at home. The powerful shower jets gave me some relief from the excruciating pain in my neck. When I got out of the shower I couldn't find any of my clothes in my bedroom. Dermot was in the living room playing on the Xbox.

'Where are my clothes?' I asked him. 'What have you done with my clothes?'

He pointed to the smaller second bedroom which I had been using as a study.

'I moved them in there for you,' he said cheerfully. 'My suits will be arriving in the morning.'

'But ... but ... you've taken my bedroom?'

'Yes, I have,' he said. 'The waterbed must have been playing havoc with your neck. I'm sure you'll feel much better after a good night's sleep on the sofabed in there.'

There was no point in arguing. There was never any point in arguing with Dermot. Anyway, I knew my basic needs were catered for in the smaller room and none of Dermot's needs could be described as basic. He is probably allergic to a lack of luxury.

For dinner Dermot and I shared the turkey, a tin of lentils and some fizzy water. I hadn't expected to be in the apartment over Christmas.

The next morning Dermot was on the phone ordering in food and drink for a party. Apparently, he had been due to host a poker game at home that day and was relocating the event to my apartment.

From mid-afternoon the Chiefs of Staff of various government departments began arriving, each one more exquisitely turned out than the next.

'What are we playing for?' I asked innocently as Dermot dealt the first hand.

'Our departmental budgets,' the Chief of Staff at the

Department of Education said happily.

'Fine by me. I don't have one,' I said, laughing. I presumed he was joking.

This caused some consternation around the table and there were questions as to whether or not I should be allowed to play. 'I know,' said Dermot, 'you can bet portions of the loan.'

Obviously I was reluctant to get involved in such a dubious practice, but they were very insistent and I fancied my chances as I had put myself through college playing poker. As it turned out my opponents weren't very good at the game and within two hours I had won the budgets for a new prison, two intensive care units, a cancer treatment centre of excellence and a university research department.

'You know, I really don't want any of this,' I said during a break from the game. 'Couldn't you just keep the money and provide the services?'

Everyone looked at me, completely aghast.

'We couldn't possibly,' said Dermot. 'You must have a very low opinion of us.'

Everyone around the table glared at me as I tried to rescue the situation.

'Far from it,' I said. 'I've just had a great time. This is the best ... what do you call it on this side of the Atlantic? Oh yes – Boxing Day. This is the best Boxing Day I can remember and I'd feel bad taking the money after such a great afternoon.'

A grim silence descended on the room. Nobody talked to me as one by one they got their coats and left.

They shook their heads in sorrow as they bade farewell to Dermot at the door.

'What did I do?' I asked Dermot. 'Was it something I said?'

He wouldn't look me in the eye as he walked to his room. 'It's St Stephen's Day,' he said as he slammed the door.

Apparently you can squander a country's wealth and blight a people's future with gleeful impunity, but never call 26 December 'Boxing Day'. Dermot didn't speak to me for several days. I still had a lot to learn about this country.

I tried several times to get into the office in the days between Christmas and New Year but Government Buildings were like a ghost town. They were lonely days. Dermot ignored me as he sat for hours playing on the Xbox, eating Cadbury's Roses and Marks & Spencer vol au vents straight from the packet.

Then suddenly and mysteriously I was forgiven. Dermot called me from my room with tears in his eyes. 'Come on,' he said, 'we're going to the office.'

'We won't be able to get in,' I said. 'I tried yesterday. There's nobody at work.'

'It will be open,' he said. 'This isn't work. This matters.'

A small group of civil servants had gathered under the portrait of former Taoiseach and Finance Minister Bertie Ahern where it hung in Dermot's office in the Department of Finance. One by one they placed offerings under the portrait and whispered prayers. Candles were lit on the makeshift shrine and there were some garlands of flowers. Most of the offerings, however, were simple brown envelopes.

'It's a tradition,' Dermot told me.

On the way to the office, he had explained that Mr Ahern had announced that he would not contest the upcoming general election. 'It's the end of an era,' he said.

'We worshipped him,' Dermot told me, as we stood beneath the portrait. 'We felt he was one of us; he had no respect for anything.'

'He had an instinct for how government worked,' he continued. 'He would set up a new inquiry or tribunal at the drop of a hat. He didn't look for results – he knew better than that. Nothing fazed him. You know what?' Dermot turned to face me. 'If he was still our leader the whole country would have celebrated bringing in the IMF. He would have made it seem like the best thing to happen to Ireland since independence. We would have welcomed you with great festivities. Bertie would have announced a bank holiday for your arrival and arranged a parade on an open-top bus. Bertie loved bank holidays. He had style.'

While Dermot was talking I could hear other civil servants paying tribute to Bertie as they placed their gifts under the portrait. Some of them scrawled personal messages on the brown envelopes. 'We'll never forget you, the leader of the pack,' one note read.

Department of Finance officials were weeping openly. 'You know he didn't even have a bank account? He didn't believe in money,' one of them said to me. 'That became our philosophy too. We learned so much from him. He was a saint.'

'He was a socialist,' another man said.

'He was superb,' Dermot said. 'When he left the Department we escorted him to the door with a guard of honour. When we went back inside, everything was gone. Desks, computers, carpets, light fittings, wallpaper. I mean everything. We looked up every tree in Drumcondra for them. We couldn't search his house though – he didn't have one. None of it was ever found. He must have made everything miraculously appear in the office of a poor civil servant in Calcutta or some such awful place. Athlone maybe. He was that type of man. Material goods meant nothing to him.'

Suddenly my eyes were drawn to an older gentleman sobbing quietly to himself. Dermot said he was a retired Chief of Staff of the Department. 'Look,' the old man said suddenly. 'The portrait just sighed and raised its eyebrows. It's a miracle!'

Dermot immediately announced that he would organise a petition to have Bertie beatified. From now on no major decisions were to be taken in the Department of Finance without first consulting the portrait of Bertie the Good.

Later, as we walked back to the apartment, Dermot was in unusually reflective form. 'You know,' he said reverentially. 'Bertie could make a pint of Bass appear without putting his hand in his pocket. We'll miss him.'

~FIVE~

THE ODD COUPLE

✿ ✿ ✿ ✿ ✿ ✿ ✿ ✿ ✿ ✿ ✿ ✿ ✿ ✿ ✿ ✿ ✿ ✿ ✿

Dermot started the New Year as he hoped to continue. On our first day back after the Christmas break, he sent out a memo to all staff informing them that they would receive a 10 per cent windfall bonus because tax revenues for the fourth quarter of 2010 exceeded expectations by a fraction of a per cent. I found out about the ridiculous memo when I noticed a commotion as staff members emerged from their usual inertia to congratulate each other on a job well done. One man actually lifted his head off his desk for the first time since I had been there. As they high-fived each other, whooped and whistled and went on eBay to spend their newfound riches, Liam told me about the contents of the memo.

'Can I do a Reply All on that?' I asked him. I was still getting to grips with SuperSpaceMail2000, the Department of Finance email program.

'Of course you can. It's just like Outlook,' Liam said helpfully.

'Why don't you just use Outlook, like the rest of the civilised world?' I asked him.

Liam looked slightly worried, as though he was afraid someone might overhear our conversation. 'We really should,' he said, all the while looking anxiously around the room, 'but Dermot insisted that we had to have our own system because the Department of Justice use Outlook and he thought it looked boring. It sort of does the same thing as Outlook, except not as well. You can make your emails pink or yellow though.'

'Oh,' I said. 'I should have known.'

I typed my brief message:

'As some of you may have heard, your economy has been the subject of an IMF-EU bailout to the tune of €85 billion. With that in mind, and despite any other information you may have received, there will be no bonuses paid to Department of Finance staff unless authorised by me acting for Ajai Chopra and the IMF. This is extremely unlikely to happen any time soon.'

The news spread quickly, as did the murmurs of disapproval when the staff realised the implication of the memo. Gradually they returned to their desks and their slumbers. Several civil servants approached me and offered me enticements to change my mind. Within the space of a few minutes I was offered four houses on ghost estates and three time-share apartments in Spain. I'm not sure they understood the principle of bribery – the bribe should at least have a value.

Dermot, of course, was livid. 'I want those bonuses reinstated,' he demanded.

'Under no circumstances,' I said. 'We are far removed

from bonus territory, Dermot. You have to make serious changes to how things operate here before any kind of bonus could even be considered.'

'Excuse me! We operate perfectly well,' he said. 'We've imposed all the cuts you wanted in the Budget. What more do you want? Blood from a stone? Feathers from a frog?'

'We want to see that you can manage your economy,' I said. 'There is no point in us bailing you out if you come back looking for more money in six months' time. We want you to slash spending on all but the most essential services and then maintain those services while imposing further cuts wherever you can.'

'Well that won't be hard,' said Dermot. 'Services are rubbish here anyway. We could get rid of the Departments of Health and Education for a start.'

'You see no benefit in the continued existence of your Departments of Health and Education?' I said, aghast. Even by Dermot's standards this was staggering.

'Well, of course not,' he said. 'Apart from the obvious benefit, and only real purpose, of providing jobs for people.

'How can you say that?'

'How could I not?' he said. 'Look at Education. We have one of the most highly educated workforces in Europe but 25 per cent of them are illiterate. And the rest of them got top grades because of our policy of grade inflation. As for Health, I've never seen the point of it. I mean, we're supposed to get sick and die aren't we?'

'So are there any government departments you would keep?'

'Ah, sure you'd have to have a few,' Dermot said. 'We'd

be lost without Finance, wouldn't we?' he winked knowingly at me. 'And Justice is vital, otherwise the prisons would be empty. There wouldn't be much point in paying all those prison officers if there were no prisoners, now would there? Any fool can see that.'

I looked across the office at the man who spent every working moment fast asleep with his head on his desk. I was beginning to understand that his might well be the only rational response to working at the Department of Finance under Dermot Mulhearn.

'You're unbelievable, Dermot,' I said. 'But you're still not getting those bonuses.'

'To hell with you,' he said. 'We can default. All I have to do is say the word.'

I couldn't contain a bitter laugh.

'You probably will default on the bank debts. And you wouldn't even be paying those if you had the courtesy to negotiate with your European friends in 2008 before you sent Lenihan out to guarantee the deposits. But if you don't play ball with us, Dermot, you'll have no money to run the country. You have nowhere else to turn.'

Dermot wasn't happy. He checked the time on his Rolex.

'I can't stand around here gossiping with you,' he said. 'There is work to be done. I have a Finance Department to run. I'm going for a cappucino.'

I hurried home immediately after work to get a few precious moments of peace in the apartment before Dermot turned up. His domestic habits are in sharp contrast to the suave image he presents to the world. The sitting room floor was littered with his dirty socks and discarded crisp packets. There was rotting food down the side of the couch and cereal blocking the kitchen sink. Despite having his own en suite Dermot regularly relieves himself in the main bathroom. To be honest I'm not sure he even aims for the toilet. In fairness he does clean up his splashes – I just wish he wouldn't use my towel to do it. I now drink my coffee black as Dermot simply doesn't understand that milk is kept in the fridge and not beside the radiator. If only he would pay some rent we would be able to afford a cleaner.

I broached the subject of rent with him on several occasions. 'Don't you see my hands are tied?' he said. 'I can't pay rent to my wife while my solicitor is telling her solicitor that I am completely overextended. Surely you understand that?'

I could see his logic but it grated that as he explained this to me he was drinking a glass of Romanée-Conti that must have cost €1,500 a bottle.

'Perhaps if you bought cheaper wine?' I suggested.

'Don't be so silly. You don't really think I would be relying on your kindness while going out and spending a fortune on wine, do you? What must you think of me? I didn't buy this. It was a gift from the Department,' he said.

Dermot's wife collected the rent from me in person.

She is an intimidating woman, about six foot tall and probably bulletproof. She has the look of Cruella De Vil about her, only orange.

'Just do exactly what she tells you to do,' Dermot told me before she was due to call for the first time. 'Don't look her in the eye and don't make any sudden movements.'

'You make her sound like some kind of wild animal,' I said.

'Have you seen *Alien vs Predator?*'

'Yes,' I said, becoming a little nervous.

'She's sort of like Predator – but in couture. Let's just leave it at that,' he said and went to hide in his room.

When I opened the door, she looked me up and down for a very long minute.

'So you're the man with the money,' she said with a sneer. 'You don't look it.'

'Those that look it spend it,' I said, trying to hold my nerve. 'We like to hang onto it.'

'We like to hang onto it,' she mimicked in a grotesque high-pitched sing-song voice. 'Well you're not hanging on to mine,' she thundered. 'There are two of you living here now and I want an extra €600 per month. There'll be a double deposit for Dermot. I know he'll ruin the place with his filthy habits.'

'That's out of the question,' I said.

Sinéad stepped forward, sandwiching me between her breasts and the wall. I could feel the pressure on my chest as she leaned into me. There was more give in the wall than in her breasts. 'There are no questions, only instructions,' she

said in a low whisper as she ground the heel of her stilletto
into my foot. The pain in my foot competed with the pain in
my neck, which had increased dramatically since meeting
Sinéad. She put her index finger under my chin and lifted
my head so that our eyes met. 'No late payments,' she said.
She stepped back and I slumped slightly almost as a reflex
action. She studied me coolly from a few feet away like a
cat deciding how to disembowel a trapped mouse. I noticed
her skin was the same burnt-orange colour as Dermot's, but
whereas his had the smooth texture of a luxurious couch,
hers was so tough and weathered by the sun that it might still
be on the cow.

'Where's Dermot?' she asked, with a troubling glint in
her cold eyes.

'He's out,' I told her.

'You're lying,' she said and pushed me out of the way.
'DERMOT!' she screamed.

He was locked in his room and we had agreed he
wouldn't come out under any circumstances. But almost
immediately upon hearing Sinéad screech his name,
Dermot appeared at the door.

'Is everything OK, Sinéad?' he asked nervously, looking only at the floor.

Sinéad emitted a harsh laugh.

'Is he always so frisky with the ladies?' she asked
Dermot, all the while staring at me, threatening me to
defend myself.

'How dare you?' I said. 'I have been nothing but a
gentleman.'

'You've been nothing but a loser. As if you'd know what to do with a woman!'

Dermot was still staring sheepishly at the floor. 'Don't be mean to him Sinead. He's my friend. And he's a guest of the nation.'

She laughed for an uncomfortable amount of time. 'Your friend?' she said. 'You are pathetic. You and your boyfriend are both pathetic. Dermot, you have the kids this weekend. I don't want to catch sight nor sound of them until Monday morning.'

With that she turned on her heel and left.

It took us a while to get over that. We sat side-by-side on the couch playing *Red Dead Redemption* on the Xbox for hours, without talking.

I rarely got to spend any time alone in the apartment without Dermot. I think he knew that Ajai had told me to keep an eye on him so he insisted that every social occasion was work related. Sometimes out of sheer exhaustion I cried off, but I usually felt so guilty afterwards that it wasn't worth it.

He and his colleagues had an endless appetite for the social whirl. They never seemed tired or hungover, and, of course, it didn't interfere with work because they didn't really do any. I on the other hand had to monitor spending across all government departments and ensure that all cuts were being implemented. And I was still dosing myself with Valium and Difene. I was burning the candle at both ends and it was catching up with me.

On a few occasions Dermot had to wake me for work.

I have never before needed an alarm clock and have never been anything less than punctual. I would wake from a troubled sleep to find Dermot standing over me.

'Wake up, dear boy, we have a country to save,' he would say, shaking my shoulder and usually spilling cereal on my duvet at the same time. I would gradually wake up to find him beautifully turned out in the finest tailoring, smelling of aftershave and fresh coffee. He tried to get me to order a suit from Louis Copeland when, due to the rich food I had been eating, I found that I needed to go up a couple of sizes. I declined and said I'd try the Bargain Shop in Arnotts. He looked genuinely horrified. 'I'm not sure they'll let you in there without a pram,' he told me.

Three times that week Ajai had phoned me in work before I got there. He didn't raise the issue. He didn't have to. I knew that he wasn't impressed and he knew that I knew he wasn't impressed. Worse still, Dermot knew that I knew that Ajai wasn't impressed. 'Don't worry, we'll always look after you here,' Dermot said, like the spider to the fly.

But I did worry. I worried when I woke and I worried when I slept. I worried about Ajai. I worried about the Irish economy and I worried about Dermot and the Finance Minister. One night I took an extra Valium to help me sleep and woke in the middle of the night to find Dermot and Mary Coughlan in my room, dressed as dentists. The Minister for Education and Skills was holding me in a dentist's chair. Her grip was vice-like. I couldn't move a muscle as Dermot cheerfully came towards me with a Black & Decker drill.

'We couldn't find the normal one,' he said with a frown.

'Never mind. This won't hurt at all. Now, tell me, is it safe?'
he asked.

'Is what safe?' I replied, confused and disoriented. He
drilled deep into one of my teeth and I screamed in unbear-
able agony.

'Is it safe?' he asked again drilling further into my tooth,
but somehow knowing to stop before I fainted.

'Is what safe?' I screamed.

'The money, you muppet,' Dermot said and they both
laughed wildly.

I woke up bathed in sweat. The room was empty. Even
in my sleep I couldn't escape Dermot and his friends. And
strangely, in addition to my neck pain and my wounded foot
where Sinead had ground her heel into it, I was also suffering from a severe toothache. Can dreams do that?

I continued to work quietly at my desk during the day while
the rest of the office drifted along waiting for the next bit of
excitement. Their days were usually spent scanning media
websites and Twitter to see what new scandal was breaking
in government circles or in Cheryl Cole's life. A government
scandal was rarely a surprise to them because they generally leaked the story in the first place. But when it came to
Cheryl there could be hours of speculation over her latest
row with Ashley.

In quiet times between news stories the staff could

become quite bitter and introspective. At times like these Dermot and his colleagues were actually inclined to do a bit of work. The 'work' however was generally focussed on purposeless projects conceived only to amuse the staff themselves. They might cancel a project just as it was ready to report and then announce a new one to replace it, or they might suddenly transfer some staff to new offices and then transfer them back as soon as they got settled in. Of course these foolish things cost money. They ate away at any savings made through the cutbacks.

These apparently random initiatives often started as simple office bullying. The decentralisation project was a good example. It was pure folly, and it cost a fortune, but Liam told me it was only introduced because Dermot hated having to rub shoulders with civil servants from the Department of Social Welfare. When I asked Dermot about it he was unrepentant. 'They dressed like they were on welfare themselves, in their Jesus sandals and Aran jumpers,' he told me. 'I had to do something. I simply couldn't look at them.'

Shortly after Christmas the media and the opposition went into overdrive over undisclosed contact between Mr Cowen and Sean Fitzpatrick before the banking guarantee was announced in September 2008. Apparently they played golf and had dinner together. Mr Cowen insisted in the Dáil that they didn't discuss the bank's business at all that day. Of course at first this sounds absurd to any reasonable person, but it ended up being totally believeable, as I briefed Ajai after the Taoiseach spoke.

'You're saying there's nothing to worry about?' Ajai asked.

'No, I'm not saying that, Mr Chopra. There's always something to worry about here. What I am saying is there is probably nothing sinister to worry about. I have spent some time with the Taoiseach, and ridiculous as it may seem, it is actually entirely believable that he and Mr Fitzpatrick didn't discuss Anglo.'

'But why else would they meet except to talk about the bank?' Ajai asked. 'What the hell did they talk about?'

'They probably told jokes, did a few impressions and sang songs,' I said.

'My God,' said Ajai. 'That's worse. Are you sure?'

'Pretty sure,' I said. I decided not to tell Ajai that the Taoiseach's impression of him was actually very good.

The media were calling it Golfgate and, naturally, Dermot found it all very entertaining. 'I've played golf with them loads of times,' he said. 'They only ever talk shite. Keith Barry couldn't retrieve a memory of either of them saying anything interesting.'

Meanwhile, Dermot was also excited by a speculative newspaper article suggesting that the EU might consider lowering the interest rate on the bailout money. 'I told you I was right not to go to the negotiations,' he said. 'I have the EU negotiating with themselves now. Sure we mightn't have to pay them back at all. You see there was method to my madness!'

He looked annoyed when I smirked at him. 'What are you doing here anyway?' he asked me then. 'Shouldn't you be on your way to Portugal for their bailout?'

'I should be so lucky. Portugal isn't getting a bailout,' I said.

Dermot laughed so hard that I feared for his well-being. 'No,' he said. 'Of course it isn't.'

All the talk was that Mr Cowen would have to go because of the game of golf. It obviously doesn't help in a bailout situation to have that level of political instability but we had dealt with worse. The staff were highly energised by the whole affair. I think they were keen that there might be a reshuffle and they could get a new Finance Minister to taunt.

'Oh that won't happen before the election,' Dermot said sadly. 'Mind you, you can't beat the first few weeks of a new minister. They are exquisite.'

There was something about the way he said it, as though the new Finance Minister would be a lamb to the slaughter and the slaughter would be protracted, painful and without purpose. In any event excitement was mounting at the prospect of a heave against Mr Cowen. It wasn't helped by the fact that Dermot ordered Redbull for everyone and handed round my Difene.

'I hope you enjoy the distraction,' I said to Dermot. 'It will help take your mind off the parlous state of your economy.'

Dermot laughed heartily. 'You do my heart good,' he

said. 'You really do. Who in their right mind would waste their time thinking about the economy?'

More than anyone else, Dermot was enjoying the death throes of the government. He had the Finance Minister in a state of utter confusion with his mind games. He was entertaining himself by trying to persuade Mr Lenihan to challenge for the Fianna Fáil leadership.

'Your country needs you, Minister,' he said to him, almost as though he meant it. Poor Mr Lenihan got quite worked up with boundless patriotism and was on the verge of announcing his candidacy when Dermot questioned his sense of loyalty.

'Perhaps your Taoiseach needs you,' said Dermot quietly.

Mr Lenihan stopped in his tracks. 'My Taoiseach,' he said fervently. 'I should support my Taoiseach.'

'But your country … ' said Dermot.

'My country,' said the Finance Minister, and he again prepared to contact the media to declare his position.

But Dermot continued toying with him.

'Your Taoiseach,' he said again with an evil glint in his eye.

'My Taoiseach *and* my country,' Mr Lenihan sobbed. I saw he was about to explode, but at that very moment the Taoiseach wandered into the room.

'Does anyone here have any complaints about me?' asked Mr Cowen.

He had announced that he would sound out his party's TDs to get their views on his leadership.

'We're not TDs, Taoiseach,' Dermot explained to him gently.

'Right,' said the Taoiseach. 'Does anyone fancy a pint?'

Just then Mr Lenihan dropped to one knee in front of Mr Cowen.

'I am a TD,' he said, 'and my support for your leadership is firm and unwavering, Taoiseach.'

'That's nice, Brian,' said the Taoiseach. 'Pint?'

The Taoiseach saw me at my desk and strolled over with his hand outstretched. 'Brian Cowen, Taoiseach,' he introduced himself. 'Can I rely on your support in the confidence vote? Feel free to say no. In fact please do say no.'

I couldn't believe that the Taoiseach didn't remember me, although I suppose I hadn't really encountered him in a work context, or a sober context for that matter.

'Sadly Taoiseach, I don't have a vote. I'm with the IMF, you see,' I said.

'Of course you are,' he said. 'You know I have been here too long. Everyone is starting to look like a backbencher on the make to me. I'm not even sure that I recognise myself any more. Good man yourself. You're the man with our future in the palm of his hand, eh? Are you being taken care of here? Call me if you need anything. Better hurry up though!' he said and winked at me.

'That was cruel,' I said to Dermot after the two politicians had left. 'Mr Lenihan clearly trusts you. It was wrong to toy with him like that.'

'Nonsense!' said Dermot. 'Toying with ministers is a time-honoured tradition. What else would we do with them?'

I worked late that night. Dermot was meeting Sinéad to see if they could iron out their differences, so I didn't have to be with him for a change. Apparently he had promised his children, John and Edward, that he would try to persuade Sinéad to give the marriage another chance.

'What's your plan?' I asked him before he went to meet her.

'I'm going to be strong,' he said. 'I am going to stand my ground and insist that it's my way or the highway. What do you think?'

'I think the bailout has a better chance of succeeding,' I said.

'Oh,' said Dermot. 'Should I beg? I should beg, shouldn't I?'

'That might be wise,' I said, 'and it's good practice for the future.'

I left the Department of Finance at around eleven o'clock and heard a voice from the shadows as I passed the Department of the Taoiseach. 'Come all ... come all ye ...,' a voice wracked with sobs attempted to sing.

'Is that you, Taoiseach?' I asked as I peered into the darkness.

'Ah, my friend from the IMF,' he said. 'My friend from the IMF, would you like to be Taoiseach? You'd make a great job of it. Sure Dev was a Yank. You'd hardly be any worse than him.' Suddenly he looked around with a panicked expression on his face.

'I didn't say that. You didn't hear that. The last thing I need is for someone to hear me criticising Dev. So what do you think? Would you like to be Taoiseach? All of this could be yours.' He swung his arm expansively, indicating his impressive office.

'No, thank you, Taoiseach,' I said. 'Between you and me I'm not a big fan of parliamentary democracies. They're very hard to control.'

Mr Cowen shrugged. I'm not sure that he actually heard me.

'No one wants to be Taoiseach,' he said. 'I never wanted the job either, you know. I was perfectly happy being Minister for Finance, doing what they told me to do. I always did what I was told – and look where it got me! Where did it all go wrong?'

'Maybe you picked the wrong advisers,' I suggested.

'Picked them?! I didn't pick them. They picked themselves. I wouldn't know where to start.

'Would you believe that I just won a vote of confidence in my leadership and here I am talking to a stranger? No offence,' he said.

'None taken, Taoiseach,' I assured him.

'I won it,' he said, as though he couldn't believe it. 'I never saw that coming. Micheál Martin should be sitting here now, sad and alone talking to a bloody Yank. No offence.'

Again I assured him that I didn't take any offence. I could see how upset he was at winning the confidence vote. His success had crushed him.

'You wouldn't have voted for me, would you? What were they thinking? Now Martin has resigned. It's easy for him.

He's in there with the rest of them joking and laughing and blaming me for everything we all did together. Making out I'm nothing but a pub singer. I wasn't singing on my own, you know. They all joined in on the chorus. I'm going to show them though. I am going to resign. That'll show them.'

'Are you serious, Taoiseach?' I asked.

'Never more so,' he said. 'They might have confidence in me but I certainly don't. I have no confidence in them either. It's over. Don't tell anyone, though. I want it to be a surprise for the feckers.'

'Your secret is safe with me, Taoiseach,' I said. 'My lips are sealed.'

I resolved to email Ajai on my Blackberry as soon as I got away from him.

'Do you know,' he paused for a moment. 'The worst part of being Taoiseach has been dealing with bankers. I see more of them now than I did when I was Finance Minister. They're a dry shower of shites, do you know that? They laugh at you not with you, and they don't respect a song. I don't think they have it in them to respect a song. Imagine! Come on, we'll sing a song! Do you know this one?' The Taoiseach cleared his throat and started singing. 'I knew Danny Farrell when his football was a can ....'

I stayed a while but slipped away without him noticing. I liked the Taoiseach but I needed my sleep. Someone had to get up in the morning and run the country.

I hadn't seen Dermot for a few days. His meeting with Sinéad had gone better than expected and he had taken her on a weekend break to a spa hotel. I declined his invitation to join them.

'We're publishing the Finance Bill this week, remember?' I said to him.

'Oh, that thing,' he said dismissively. 'You'll be fine with that. You don't need me,' he said. 'Why don't you cover for me and I'll try to bring you back a nice bathrobe?'

I told Dermot how I had found the Taoiseach all alone in his office, without mentioning his plans to resign, but he didn't seem surprised.

'Their careers always end badly. They have no solid foundations – kind of like the economy!' He thought this was a hilarious comparison. 'Did you see this?' he asked as he handed me a newspaper article reporting that the Irish Central Bank was printing its own money. 'You may as well go back to Washington,' he said. 'We're printing our own money now. We don't need you.'

It was typical of Dermot's sense of humour.

'That's nice,' I replied. 'Have you tried spending any of it yet?'

Ajai phoned after Dermot had left. He liked the presentation on the National Recovery Plan that I wrote for Dermot. I was chuffed.

'How is everything there?' he asked.

'Oh, it's fine, Mr Chopra. We're working away on the Finance Bill but there is a chance that the political instability here could delay it.'

'Don't let that happen,' Ajai said, as though I could somehow arrest the collapse of a government that was hell-bent on its own destruction. 'But if it does you will be coming home and bringing the bailout money with you.'

I would enjoy passing that information on to Dermot.

Dermot came back a day early from his spa break. He would have looked ashen if his face wasn't the colour of a sunset.

'What happened to you?' I asked him.

'The bitch locked me in the tanning machine,' he said bitterly. 'I'm completely the wrong colour. I'm going to have to change my entire wardrobe. Nothing matches.'

Although he was upset that Sinéad had tricked him I could tell he was suffering from a deeper malaise.

'What else is wrong, Dermot?' I asked him. I had expected him to be energised by the fact that no less than five government ministers, including his beloved Mary Harney, had resigned in the space of a couple of days.

'Follow me,' he said and he led me to the room Liam had called the Harney Room. Dermot looked quite emotional as he put the key in the door and turned it. 'I've never shown anyone else this room,' he said. 'You may have noticed my regard for our Minister for Health, or should I say our former Minister for Health. I always cherished the hope that Mary Harney would one day be Finance Minister. Now that hope is gone,' he said sadly. 'I kept this room ready for her just in case.'

Dermot showed me into the most sumptuous room I have ever been in. There was a beautiful conference table with what I can only describe as a throne at the head of it.

There was a magnificent fireplace, and, to my astonishment, the fire was lit. Dermot noticed my gaze. 'I kept the fire going all day every day,' he said. 'She often arrived unannounced. Mary would have liked it here,' Dermot leaned on the throne. He looked like he might start crying. 'I kept it for her ever since Bertie left Finance. No one else was worthy. But it wasn't meant to be.'

Dermot sat on the throne, looking dejected.

'It suits you,' I said, trying to lighten the mood. 'Perhaps you should become Minister for Finance.'

'Perhaps I should,' he said. 'Perhaps I should indeed.'

Dermot was lost in thought for a few moments, but then he jumped up off the throne and seemed to be immediately back in good spirits.

'You should be delighted Mary Harney is stepping down,' he said. 'It will save a fortune on fuel. Maybe even enough to pay you lads back.'

'How would that be possible, Dermot?' I asked.

'Mary had a sort of unspoken authority. We did things for her that we would not have contemplated for any other minister. Fuel was just one of them. We left the engines running on the government jet, the helicopters, her ministerial car. Anything we thought she might want to use. She had a habit of just turning up, wanting to go somewhere, and we would never keep her waiting.'

'You kept a jet on the runway with its engines running?'

'Yes, we did. Twenty-four hours a day, seven days a week, for years and years. There was something about Mary,' he said.

As we left the Harney Room we ran into the Finance

Minister with his aunt, who was holding him by the hand. 'My nephew didn't get a double ministry,' she said sharply to Dermot. 'O'Cuiv has so many jobs he falls asleep trying to remember them and my nephew is still only the Minister for Finance,' she hissed.

'What are you talking about, Mammy?' Dermot asked her.

'Bloody Gormley wouldn't let Cowen appoint new ministers,' she protested. 'So he gave all the jobs to existing ministers. My Brian got nothing!'

'Oh, that is disappointing, Mary, but don't worry,' said Dermot brightly. 'That gives us more time to focus on a leadership challenge, doesn't it?'

The Minister for Finance just looked confused.

~SIX~

BUNGA BUNGA

☆☆☆☆☆☆☆☆☆☆☆☆☆☆☆☆

I had my longest ever conversation with Ajai on Skype a few days later. After he hung up I realised we had been talking for nearly four minutes. Naturally he wanted a briefing on the state of play with the Government and whether it would last long enough for the Finance Bill to be passed.

'It's impossible to call at the moment,' I said. 'Lenihan wants to delay the election until March so the bill can be passed. He says it won't be possible to pass it before then.'

'What about the opposition?' Ajai asked.

'They're threatening a vote of no confidence if the election isn't brought forward. They think the bill can be passed sooner.'

'Where does Cowen stand on all this?'

'To be honest I think he's stepped down in all but name,' I said. 'He's gone back to his constituency, supposedly to discuss his plans with his family.'

'Supposedly?'

'Well, the rumours are bad, Mr Chopra,' I said.

'Spit it out.'

'People are saying that he hasn't been singing. The rumour is that he said he'd never sing again.'

There was a silence as Ajai digested this information. 'OK,' he said finally, 'so Mr Cowen is yesterday's man. What about the other fella? What's his name? Kenny.'

'He seems to have been sent into hiding,' I said. 'His people are all gung ho, though. His finance guy, Michael Noonan, turns up on every news bulletin.'

'Noonan,' said Ajai. 'Is that the creepy one?'

'That's him. He's everywhere but there's no sign of Kenny.'

'Makes sense. Kenny isn't the most impressive character.'

'What about Dermot? How are you getting on with him? Is he buying into austerity for Ireland?'

'He has no problems with austerity for Ireland,' I assured Ajai, 'as long as it doesn't mean austerity for Dermot. Other people's poverty doesn't bother him in any way.'

'That's not entirely unreasonable,' said Ajai. 'Keep a tight leash on him. If we have some sort of control over him we have a chance of preventing the new government from doing anything stupid.'

'OK, Mr Chopra,' I said. 'But if you rule out stupid you don't leave them much room to manouevre.'

'Don't I know it!' Ajai replied and hung up.

The following morning, a Saturday, I was enjoying a lie-in when Dermot burst into the room. 'Come on,' he said. 'We're going to work.'

'It's Saturday, Dermot,' I groaned.

'I know what day it is,' Dermot said. 'The Taoiseach's driver just phoned me. Mr Cowen is going to announce he's standing down. We have to go to work now.'

'Oh, right, of course,' I said. 'We'd better reassure the EU, the ECB and Ajai that everything is under control.'

'Whatever,' said Dermot. 'They can figure that out for themselves. We have to make sure that Mr Lenihan secures the Fianna Fáil leadership.'

'Whatever for? That's a party political matter. It has nothing to do with us.'

Dermot was aghast. 'Nothing to do with us? It would be a black day in the Department of Finance if a Minister for Foreign Affairs became Taoiseach. Even if it is only for a few days. They're not fit to run a country. They're not fit for anything other than handing out Ferrero Rocher. And my department pays for the Ferrero Rocher.'

Dermot spent the morning writing a speech for the Minister, who had been persuaded by his aunt and Dermot to throw his hat in the ring for the leadership. Dermot worked feverishly, hunched over a page, deep in concentration. His seemingly intense efforts made it all the more surprising when I saw the product of his labours. There were four short lines.

1. Strength of character
2. Courage of my convictions
3. Good communicator
4. Inspirational leader

'Is that it?' I asked. 'Has he nothing tangible to offer?'

'Any more than that would leave him hopelessly confused,' Dermot said. 'Anyway, they're Lenihan buzzwords. As long as he says them with his trademark fervour, the parliamentary party will go mad for it.'

The prospect of becoming leader of Fianna Fáil caused the Minister to question his relationship with Dermot. He told Dermot he didn't want him to stand beside him when he announced his candidacy. Dermot was very annoyed, having worked so hard on the Minister's speech. I think that's why he booked the Banking Hall in the Westin Hotel for the press conference. Mr Lenihan didn't seem to notice the journalists sniggering at the choice of location. He didn't seem to notice them sniggering at the very idea of his candidacy either.

'Minister,' said one journalist snidely, 'do you not think your candidacy will be compromised by your disastrous record in managing the banking crisis?'

'I believe I have shown great strength of character and inspirational leadership in managing the banking crisis,' Mr Lenihan replied.

'Do you recall saying that the bailout would be the cheapest in the world?' the journalist asked with a smug grin.

'Yes, well,' said Mr Lenihan, 'I acted on the best advice available to me. Sadly some of that advice turned out to be flawed.'

The Minister stared pointedly at Dermot as he said this and I could see that Dermot could barely contain his anger. The sooner Ireland got a new government the better as there was no longer a functioning relationship between

the Department of Finance and the Minister – not, I had
to admit, that it had been functioning that well in the first
place.

Everyone at Government Buildings was preoccupied
with the Fianna Fáil leadership contest. My requests for documents relating to departmental expenditure were ignored
as the staff concentrated on inventing and spreading gos-
sip via Twitter and Facebook. However, Liam and another
clerical officer impressed me hugely with their discipline in
the face of such distraction. They ignored all the fuss and
worked non-stop, shredding documents.

Meanwhile the opposition parties' demand for an early
election led to their finance spokespeople coming to the
Department to meet with the Minister. They were insisting
that the Finance Bill could be passed more speedily than Mr
Lenihan had suggested. Of course Dermot was delighted to
be hosting them and laid on canapés and drinks for them.
He was disgusted, however, when they ignored his presence
and his efforts and made straight for Mr Lenihan's office.

'Ah, Ms Burton,' Dermot said as the Labour spokeswoman passed him by, 'you are very welcome to the
Department of Finance. We are going to do our absolute
best to see if we can formulate an actual policy for you and
your excitable friends in the Labour Party.'

Ms Burton was well able for him, however. 'Honesty is
the best policy, Mr Mulhearn,' she said. 'And I am honestly
not about to listen to you. If only Mr Lenihan had done the
same, the country might not be in the gutter.'

As she spoke, she gripped Michael Noonan's elbow and

brought him into the conversation.

'I don't think there's any need for Dermot to attend this meeting, do you, Michael?' she said.

Mr Noonan walked over to Dermot and fixed him with beady eyes.

'You remind me of a weasel,' he said, 'like Richard Bruton. Or perhaps ye are both snakes, without any backbone at all. I wouldn't attend the meeting if I were you. In fact, don't.'

There is something quite fearsome about Mr Noonan, and Dermot, wisely I thought, kept his mouth shut for once. Mr Noonan then turned his attention to me.

'So you're the IMF fella. You should come to the meeting. You can report back to Mr Chopra that a Fine Gael government will have an entirely different style of negotiating with him and his boyos.'

I wasn't comfortable with the idea of attending the meeting, but I got the impression that I didn't have much choice in the matter. Dermot was absolutely livid. 'What are they talking to Lenihan and you for? He doesn't know anything and you're only a blow-in,' he exclaimed angrily before we went into the room without him.

To be fair to Dermot, he had a point. The Minister seemed at a loss as to how to conduct the meeting without anyone to prompt him.

'So, here we are ... yes ... well ... let me see ... would anyone like tea?' he asked in an earnest tone.

'Tea!' said Ms Burton, as though he had offered her cocaine. 'The economy is collapsing around our ears and the

Minister for Finance is making tea!'

'Milk and one sugar,' said Mr Noonan. 'Calm down and have a cup of tea, Joan. This is going to be thirsty work.'

There was an awkward few minutes of silence as Mr Lenihan waited for the kettle to boil and smiled inanely at us.

'Would anyone like a biscuit?' he said eventually. 'I have Jammie Dodgers.'

'Jammie Dodgers, is it?' said a clearly disappointed Mr Noonan. 'I suppose Rich Tea wouldn't be good enough for the likes of you.'

We all declined the offer, but the minister put a few in his pocket and returned to the table with a pot of tea and four cups.

Cup of tea in hand, Mr Noonan took charge of the meeting.

'Now, Brian,' he said, 'we need to pass this bill quickly. The public wants an election to get rid of you feckers for once and for all.'

'Yes, of course,' said Mr Lenihan.

Just then there was a knock and Dermot stuck his head around the door.

'I have an important note for the Minister,' he said. He handed a Post-it note to Mr Lenihan, winked at me and left the room. I was sitting beside Mr Lenihan and I could see that it said, in Dermot's handwriting, that it would take three weeks to pass the Finance Bill. Mr Lenihan put the note in his pocket and gravely told the opposition politicians the position according to the note from Dermot.

Just as Mr Noonan was about to respond, Dermot appeared again with another note. This one said it would take just ten days to pass the bill and Mr Lenihan dutifully relayed the new information. Clearly, Dermot was determined to exact revenge on Mr Lenihan for not standing up for him. Mr Noonan and Ms Burton raised their eyebrows and looked at each other. 'Minister,' Ms Burton began, but Dermot interrupted proceedings again and handed the Minister a third note. This one had just a smiley face drawn on it. Mr Lenihan read it, folded it, put it in his pocket and smiled at the increasingly irritated politicians across the table from him.

Two awkward minutes later, Dermot handed the Minister a note with a sad face drawn on it. Mr Lenihan read it, folded it, put it in his pocket and frowned across the table. As though to demonstrate his capacity for cruelty, the last advice note Dermot gave the Minister was blank. Mr Lenihan looked desperately confused as he looked from the note to me and back to the note. Eventually he reached a decision as to what it meant. With a look of great deliberation on his face, Mr Lenihan folded the note, put it in his pocket and looked blankly around the room. The meeting ended with the Minister sitting at the table, sweating, and Dermot looking triumphantly superior as he showed the opposition politicians out. 'Goodbye, Ms Burton,' he said. 'We will see you in due course, Mr Noonan.'

At home later that evening, Dermot was still very put out by the lack of respect the opposition politicians had shown him.

'It's all the media's fault,' he said. 'They are destroying the relationship between politicians and the civil service. Did you see that woman in the Guardian calling our competence into question? And Matt Cooper has been squeaking with indignation about us on the radio. Who is he to criticise us? He could create employment in this country by doing one job instead of three. But what does he do? He attacks poor civil servants who have no right to reply. He is trying to destroy something that has worked for generations.'

'What's that?' I asked.

'Why the natural order of things of course,' he said. 'A politician doing what a civil servant tells him. They are destroying trust. If politicians can't trust civil servants, who can they trust? Certainly not themselves.'

We were sitting on the couch watching a current affairs programme. The economist David McWilliams was explaining for the umpteenth time why Ireland should not bail out its banks. Dermot was more interested in the huge tub of Haagen Dazs ice cream he was nursing but he looked up when he heard McWilliams.

'Look at him,' he said scornfully. 'See the wink, the faint pout and the casual lick of his hyper-glossed lips? He's the economist with the sun in his hair.' Dermot spat the words out with incredible venom. 'But he won't run for public office,' he seethed. 'And he won't work in the Department of Finance. Oh no, he's a typical economist. All he wants is power without responsibility.'

'You know,' said Dermot, 'I think I should run for election. It's about time a civil servant told the truth about these economists and politicians. The public have a right to hear the truth.'

'Run? You can't run,' I said. 'You're needed where you are. You have to see through four years of austerity, if not more.'

'I might run,' Dermot said. 'I just might. The Irish people might just be ready to hear the voice of reason. And they deserve strong leadership.'

'Ajai wouldn't like it,' I said. 'He wouldn't have allowed the bailout if he didn't think you'd be there to make it succeed.'

I was working on the principle that if you're going to lie you should lie big. It didn't work.

'Well that's all very nice,' said Dermot, 'but I can't stand by while my people are cast into poverty just because Ajai wants me to. Anyway, this is bigger than Ajai. This is destiny. This is the opportunity to put the civil service at the heart of government. We could build an Ireland that will no longer tolerate gombeen politics. Civil servants, with their unquestionable integrity, will build a brave new Ireland based on the best bureaucratic principles.'

And exorbitant expense accounts, ridiculous holiday entitlements and bonuses for doing nothing, I thought, but kept my mouth shut.

Happily, Dermot didn't mention his political ambitions the next day. I was hopeful that it was just a passing fancy. While the country fretted over the state of the economy and whether or not it should default, Dermot was topping up his tan. Life went on as normal.

I was able to tell Ajai that a deal had been done on passing the Finance Bill into law. All it took was a bit of international ridicule and a few platinum buttons on the jacket of Jackie Healy-Rae's statue. The election date was set for 25 February and Dermot was unusually reflective.

'For a few weeks every five years politicians act like they don't need us,' he said. 'They go off to woo the electorate and claim credit for all the hard work us civil servants do. They are so ungrateful.'

A few days into the election campaign Dermot called a meeting of all the heads of department. I had to stay in the background as they still hadn't forgiven me for referring to St Stephen's Day as Boxing Day.

'We are all going to get shiny new ministers in a few weeks,' he told the assembled civil servants. For some of you this is new territory. The ministers will come in all eager to make a good impression. Sadly, they are incapable of such a feat. Your job is simple. Give them the impression that they've made a good impression and don't let them know that they are incapable of doing so.'

For a few days time passed in an almost orderly fashion. Many of the staff at the Department of Finance took leave to help with the Minister's re-election campaign. I thought this very unorthodox but Dermot insisted it was a time-honoured tradition to work loyally for one minister until he or she was replaced by another. The few staff who remained in the office were at a loss for something to do without a minister to brief. There was something of a holiday atmosphere as they whiled away the hours making paper aeroplanes and firing elastic bands at each other.

Meanwhile I got on with things. After examining the expense reports filed at the Department I had the unpleasant duty of informing Dermot that he had higher expenses than anyone else in the civil service or in the Dáil.

'That's right,' he said. 'And for the third year running if I say so myself.'

'Don't you think you should be setting an example?' I asked reasonably.

Dermot looked confused.

'I think I am setting an example,' he said. 'It hasn't been easy keeping ahead of the posse. I've often risked my health to head the league table.'

'The league table?' I asked, my heart sinking.

'Isn't that what we're talking about?' he asked.

'I was just going through departmental expenses for the last few years,' I said.

'Oh, there was no need for that,' he said. 'We keep a league table. It's all very transparent. The winner gets the Charles Haughey Memorial Trophy.'

Dermot took a key from his pocket and opened a cabinet on the wall behind his desk.

'See,' he said proudly. 'I get to keep it now as I've won three years in a row. I dare say it will be named after me some day.'

There was a handsome trophy and a list of names carved into a plaque on the wall. Dermot and Haughey were the only names to feature three times.

'What about austerity?' I asked. 'What about showing the public that everyone is feeling the pinch?'

'Oh, I get what you're saying,' he said, 'but I prefer to leave that kind of empty talk to the politicians. After all it really is their area of expertise. Also, life can't be all sackcloth and ashes. The suffering masses need something to aspire to. I like to think they look at me and think: *One day, if I work hard, I could be like him* … or some such nonsense.'

'Well, I'm sorry Dermot,' I said, 'but this sort of spending cannot go on. You're going to have to tighten your belt. You're living beyond your means.'

For a moment I thought he looked at me with pure hatred in his eyes, but Dermot's charm quickly took control of the situation.

'Am I indeed?' he said. 'Well, we must discuss this further. Let's chat about it in Rome.'

'In Rome? What's in Rome?'

'Such a question!' said Dermot. 'What's in Rome indeed! Why the Trevi Fountain is in Rome. The Pantheon and the Colosseum are in Rome. Not to mention the Irish rugby team and my good friend Silvio Berlusconi. Do hurry up. We mustn't keep the government jet waiting, what with austerity and all that.'

Dermot and I were the only two on the flight so I continued to press the point that I thought he needed to curtail his spending somewhat. 'If you really think so,' he said, as he licked some stray caviar from his lower lip. 'I'll look into it as soon as we get home.'

When we arrived in Rome I was surprised to see Dermot give our rugby tickets to a couple of Irish fans he met in the airport.

'We won't be needing them,' he said, looking around as though he was expecting to see somebody he knew.

'There's Anna,' he said. 'Come on. We mustn't keep Silvio waiting.'

'Silvio?' I said.

'Berlusconi,' said Dermot. 'You'll like him. He's our host for the weekend. I'm sure he'll be very interested in your ideas on frugal living.'

With that Dermot walked up to an attractive young woman wearing very short shorts and a very tight top. She also wore a chauffeur's cap at an angle on her head and was holding a sign that read 'Bunga Bunga'.

'Hello Anna,' said Dermot warmly.

'Derrrrmmmooot,' she squealed, and jumped up into his arms and smothered him in kisses. 'Derrrrmmmooot's friend,' she said then and did the same to me. In all my years with the IMF I had never felt so welcome anywhere.

'What's bunga bunga?' I asked Dermot as the delightful Anna drove us under police escort through the streets of Rome.

'You'll see,' he said.

Silvio Berlusconi greeted Dermot like a long lost son on the white marble steps of a grand villa in central Rome. The two men kissed, then hugged, then hugged, then kissed. They bore an uncanny resemblance to each other. Like father and son ... except ... it was almost as though Berlusconi had paid surgeons to make him look more like Dermot. The pair continued to embrace for several minutes before Dermot broke free and introduced me to Mr Berlusconi.

'A pleasure to meet you, sir,' I said and offered my hand.

'IMF?' said Mr Berlusconi. 'Pah!'

He slapped me across the face, turned away and walked arm in arm with Dermot into the villa. I followed at a safe distance. I was so shocked at what had just happened that it took me a few minutes to take in my surroundings. Gradually I became aware that we were not alone in the room. There were about twenty young women in various stages of undress, some lying on couches or giant cushions on the ground or writhing slowly up and down dancing poles. If that wasn't disconcerting enough, there were also three elderly men in thongs. They greeted Dermot warmly as he and Mr Berlusconi stripped down to reveal that they too were sporting thongs – matching leopardskin thongs. I backed away towards a wall holding my laptop tightly to my chest. I could feel my neck pain, which had been easing somewhat, worsen as I tensed up.

Dermot saw that I was uncomfortable and came over to me.

'Don't spoil the mood,' he said. 'Strip!'

'I don't have one of those,' I said, pointing at his thong, but trying not to look at it.

'I'll lend you one,' he said. 'In fact you can keep it.'

'I'm not wearing a thong,' I said firmly.

'Suit yourself,'

'He hit me,' I said plaintively, nodding in Mr Berlusconi's direction. 'You let him hit me.'

'I'm sorry about that,' Dermot said. 'It's just that Silvio is very protective of me. He doesn't like the idea of you being in charge of things. He didn't mean anything by it.'

'I'm not in charge of things,' I said. 'I'm just trying to help you.'

'Indeed,' said Dermot. 'Listen, you don't have to wear a thong if you don't want to but you will at least have to strip down to your underpants.'

I felt a little self-conscious in the Y-fronts I had bought in the Arnotts bargain store. I hadn't been expecting to wear them to an orgy. I hadn't expected to attend an orgy.

A short while later a bell rang and a butler, fully dressed thankfully, summoned us to dinner. Dermot and Mr Berlusconi sat with beautiful women on either side of them, as did the three elderly gentlemen. I sat alone at a distance from them with empty chairs on either side of me. Somebody was trying to make a point. One by one beautiful dishes were brought to the table. There didn't seem to be a system of starter and main course involved. Instead extravagant platters of beluga caviar, lobster, fillet of beef and veal escalope, to name but a few, were placed on the table and everyone gorged themselves as the wine flowed freely. I put my head down and concentrated on my meal when the conversation turned to the IMF's arrival in Ireland. Mr Berlusconi listened intently to Dermot's evaluation of the Irish situation.

'It's all very grim,' Dermot said. 'There's certainly no bunga bunga budget.'

'This is too sad, what you say,' said Mr Berlusconi. 'What about your politicians? Can they not tell the IMF that bunga bunga stops for no one?'

'Sadly our politicians are not men of substance like yourself,' said Dermot.

Mr Berlusconi accepted that this was likely the case and gave a slight nod.

'Then there is nothing for it my friend,' he said. 'You must become a politician. Your country needs you. Your people need bunga bunga. The IMF,' Mr Berlusconi paused, and looked down the table at me, 'clearly need bunga bunga.'

After dinner I found a quiet corner and managed to get some work done while the others drank and danced. I could see Dermot and Mr Berlusconi in the pool in the middle of the room surrounded by naked women who were competing for the men's attention. I tried to keep my gaze fixed on my laptop but it was a strange atmosphere in which to figure out how public service employment numbers kept rising even though a hiring freeze had been imposed eighteen months previously. I took the opportunity to ask Dermot about it as he passed by, doing a conga train with four naked young ladies and the Prime Minister of Italy.

'Can you explain this?' I asked him.

Dermot stopped and the conga collapsed in a writhing heap of flesh at my feet.

'How come there's more people working in the public service today than there were when you imposed the hiring freeze?'

'Oh, I advised against the hiring freeze,' said Dermot. 'People always panic and hire all their friends and family members when you introduce a freeze. But no one listens to me any more.'

Then two of the girls grabbed Dermot and he allowed himself to be led away.

'You work too hard,' he shouted over his shoulder to me. 'You should be enjoying yourself here.'

Another two girls wandered away with Mr Berlusconi, who shot a frosty look at me as he left the room. I couldn't understand his animosity. All the resentment I had expected to encounter in Ireland was instead being directed at me by the Prime Minister of Italy

Just at that moment, unfortunately, Ajai called.

'I take it you're not in the office,' Ajai said gravely.

'Ehm, no,' I said. He could obviously hear Lady Gaga playing on the stereo in the background. 'I'm in Rome with Dermot. We're being … ehm … entertained by Silvio Berlusconi.'

'Where is Dermot?' Ajai asked.

'Ehem … in a meeting, I guess,' I said.

'Well, get him back to Dublin in one piece. The wires are full of stories about Ireland defaulting. The markets don't like it. I don't like it.'

Ajai hung up.

For two days and nights Dermot and Mr Berlusconi cavorted and caroused with twenty or more women who took it in turns to dress up as nurses, police officers and, unless my eyes deceived me, some of the ministers I had met in Dublin. They played doctors and nurses, cops and robbers, a peculiar version of charades, and other games that I had not seen played before. All the while I was treated like a pariah. The young women ignored me, Mr Berlusconi glared at me and Dermot seemed oblivious to my presence.

On the third day as we were preparing to leave for the airport, I noticed that Dermot and Mr Berlusconi were engaged in deep conversation. All of the girls had been dismissed and were waiting at a distance.

The two men spoke urgently to each other in low voices. I couldn't really hear the conversation but it seemed that Dermot was seeking advice from Mr Berlusconi. Abruptly, they got up and walked towards me. I was wary after our encounter when we arrived and sank into my seat. Then they were directly in front of me, two orange-skinned men, with dyed-black hair and manicured nails, wearing matching leopardskin thongs. Once again, Mr Berlusconi slapped me across the face.

'Brutto figlio di puttana,' he said. 'Il tuo cazzo? Minuscolo!'

I'm pretty sure I could have said the same to him but I bit my tongue.

With that he was gone. I shook my head and turned to

look at Dermot. 'What the hell was that about?' I asked.

'He likes you,' he said. 'But in future you have to wear a thong.'

'Can we just go now?' I said.

Midway through the flight home I was still sitting in a corner clinging tightly to my laptop. Dermot gently eased it from my grasp and gave me a glass of wine. My hand was shaking as I raised it to my lips.

'You'll be grand,' Dermot said.

'Why didn't you ask Berlusconi to intercede on Ireland's behalf with the EU and the ECB instead of attacking me? They're the ones causing you problems,' I said.

'I did ask him,' said Dermot, 'but Silvio has his own issues with the powers that be in Europe. He wants me to meet Ghadaffi. He reckons he'd be up for buying the Irish banks and that would free us up to manage our sovereign debt.'

'Ghadaffi?' I said. 'Are you mad? You'll be international pariahs.'

'What? Like Tony Blair?' he said.

'The situation is not the same,' I said. 'It's in the optics. You'd be seen as Europe's ungrateful child, biting the hand that fed you, turning to the enemy for support.'

'That is such an American thing to say,' said Dermot. 'Assuming that someone is everyone's enemy just because they are your enemy. We Irish are friends with everyone. Even the British. Anyway, it's immaterial. I turned down Ghadaffi a couple of days before we called you lot in. His interest rate was even steeper than Trichet's. But I need to keep Silvio onside for negotiations with the EU, and he's pally with Ghadaffi so I had to look interested. You understand.'

I nodded. It seemed like the simplest thing to do.

We settled into an uneasy silence. It crossed my mind that Dermot, in a peculiar way, was always working while apparently doing nothing. And since I had met him I was always working while apparently achieving nothing.

'Silvio's a gas man, isn't he?' Dermot said out of the blue.

'He's something else,' I said.

'He told me it was my patriotic duty to take charge of my country and lead it out of the abyss, to rid my country of the IMF and lead it proudly as an independent nation,' he said.

'It's amazing what people say at an orgy,' I said.

'Isn't it?' said Dermot wistfully.

'What are you going to do?' I asked.

'I'm going to sleep on it,' he said. 'I'm exhausted.'

True to his word, Dermot slept until we landed at Dublin Airport. While he snored, I called Ajai and told him it looked increasingly likely that Dermot would run in the general election. Ajai took it surprisingly well. 'It mightn't be a bad thing to have a politician who knows how to manipulate the civil service,' he said. 'Whoever gets into power is going to have to have an efficient working relationship with the bureaucrats. Perhaps Dermot as a politician could facilitate that.'

I saw very little of Dermot in the few days after we got back from our trip to Rome. He seemed to be continually involved in hushed conversations with the heads of other departments and with his own subordinates. Then on Wednesday morning he strolled over to me with a smile on his face and showed me an article in the *Irish Times*.

'I see your boys are coming over to check up on you,' he said. I barely glanced at the article. It was standard procedure for head office to send someone over to review targets and accomplishments. 'They're not checking up on me, Dermot; they're checking up on you. I report directly to Ajai,' I said.

'Are they indeed?' he said and he turned on his heel and left.

It was the last day for election candidates to register and Dermot hadn't said another word to me about it. I was beginning to think he wasn't going to run in the general election after all.

I was wrong. Just before lunch Dermot came storming back into the office with several officials and a mob of journalists. He stood on a chair in the centre of the room and called for everyone's attention.

'Our country is in grave peril,' he said, full of importance. 'For years politicians have ignored civil service advice and exacerbated every problem we have faced. As Chief of Staff in the Department of Finance I have seen successive ministers squander our country's fortune. I am not prepared to bear witness to this economic treason any longer. I have had enough. Today I announce my candidacy in the general election. For the sake of our great nation, it is time for the civil service to run this country and lead it back to prosperity.'

'Which party are you running for?' a journalist asked.

'The party is over,' Dermot said. 'I am running as an independent candidate, affiliated to the civil service.'

'What about your job?' another journalist asked.

'A colleague will carry out my duties while I am engaged with saving the nation from the politicians,' Dermot said.

'Have you any policies?' the journalist asked.

'Of course I have policies,' Dermot said. 'I am not running for Labour. It is time for the country to learn from the self-sacrifice and commitment of the public service. It is my intention to ensure that civil service work practices and values be adopted by the private sector. There will be benchmarking for all, a minimum of thirty days' annual leave and flexi-time for retail workers.'

Dermot stepped down to rapturous applause from his colleagues and slack-jawed disbelief from the media.

I asked Dermot who was going to replace him in the Department of Finance.

'Oh, I'm just taking leave of absence,' he said. 'Liam will stand in for me if there are any decisions to be made that aren't going to be made by you.'

I looked over at Liam; he had always struck me as competent. Dermot called him over.

'You're in charge round here now, Liam,' he said. 'Do whatever our friend from the IMF says.'

'Yes sir,' said Liam.

'Oh, and one other thing Liam,' said Dermot.

'Sir?'

'You had better take a day or two off to top up your tan. We must keep up appearances.'

There was something about the way Liam agreed to this ridiculous advice from Dermot that caused me concern. I hoped he was just humouring his boss.

SEVEN

Yes We Can — Sort Of

☆ ☆

I was surprised that Dermot had selected Liam to stand in for him given that he seemed to hold him in such low regard, and I told him so when we had a moment alone.

'Oh, once Liam gets a sniff of power he'll grow into the role. You'll see. Everyone does in the end.'

I could only hope he was mistaken.

I phoned Ajai to tell him that Dermot had confirmed his candidacy in the general election and had delegated the running of the Department of Finance to Liam.

'OK,' said Ajai. 'Offer the new man your support and advice. Keep in with him but continue to keep an eye on Dermot. If he secures the backing of the civil service he could end up the most influential man in Ireland. Is it your view that Liam is likely to be a safe pair of hands?'

'Yes, Mr Chopra,' I said. 'He seems to be capable and refreshingly honest. Dermot will probably keep him on a short leash in any event.'

'Right,' said Ajai. 'You know what you have to do.'

I was running through a brief recap of my tasks when I realised that Ajai had already hung up.

Dermot decided that the Harney Room would make an ideal headquarters for his election campaign. Coffee machines, camp beds and computers were brought in by eager helpers while Dermot sat on the throne in the middle of the room, having a manicure. He looked up from his nails as the Minister for Finance walked into the room. Mr Lenihan appeared somewhat contrite and reticent. Nobody in the Department had been paying any attention to him since he had fallen out with Dermot.

'Ah, Dermot, there you are,' Mr Lenihan said as he looked around the room taking in the richness of his surroundings. 'Nice room. Is it new?'

'It's new to you, Minister,' said Dermot. 'Can I help you?'

'Yes, Dermot, you can. I seem to be at a bit of a loose end. I don't have any appointments. And there is no one pointing a camera at me. It's all very unsettling. Do you have something for me to do?'

'As a matter of fact I do, Minister,' Dermot replied. 'You should listen to me.'

The Minister clapped his hands together. 'Marvellous,' he said. 'I am all ears.'

'Good,' said Dermot. 'Minister, I have decided to stand in the general election.'

'That's great news, Dermot. Welcome to the party. We need men of your calibre in this our hour of need, when we have been dragged down by circumstances beyond our control.'

'All circumstances are beyond your control, Minister. For obvious reasons I won't be running for Fianna Fáil. I am standing as an independent.'

'Oh, well I wish you well in your endeavour. Have you picked a constituency? Do let me know if there is anything I can do.'

'I will, Minister.'

'Marvellous.'

'Minister.'

'Yes, Dermot.'

'There is something you can do.'

'Just name it, Dermot.'

'I have picked Dublin West as my constituency. I will need your help with my campaign.'

Certainly Dermot I would be only too delighted. Dublin West, eh? An interesting constituency ... much changed ... isn't it ... ahem ... isn't it mine?'

'Yes, Minister, that's why I chose it. I'm so familiar with it, you see.'

For a moment the Minister looked wary of Dermot. 'Won't we be running against each other in that case?'

'Only in a manner of speaking, Minister. I feel sure that we can unite against the common enemy that is Joan Burton, don't you?'

The Minister winced when Dermot mentioned Labour's finance spokeswoman. 'That woman has no respect for me, Dermot, no respect at all.'

'Imagine that,' said Dermot. 'As long as we remember that she is our common enemy, you and I should have no problem.'

'You're right, Dermot. I'll stand shoulder to shoulder with you and we will fight her for the last vote in Dublin West. So, where do we go from here? What is the central theme of your campaign?'

'I am basing my campaign on the need for a strong civil service. I will counter the notion that we are incompetent and out of touch with reality by revealing that we continually and consistently warned that the economy was a bubble, but that neither you nor Mr Cowen would listen to us.'

'Oh,' said Mr Lenihan 'Oh dear. Is that true? May I say Dermot that I am terribly sorry for not listening to you. It is my one regret from all my time as a public representative.'

Dermot yawned. 'Don't worry about it, Minister. Who listens to grim economic forecasts in the middle of a boom? We only filed them in case something like an economic meltdown occurred and we needed to hang you. Who knew it would happen? Apart from those cranky economists of course.'

'Oh, I see. Right you are,' said the Minister.

'Back to the matter in hand, Minister. I want you to get your election agent to contact all of your constituency workers. I need to borrow them. I can only spare a few people from the Department of Finance to help me. So many of them have taken annual leave to help with your election campaign that I'm short-staffed. I need them to get out there and replace your posters with mine.'

The Minister looked anxious but Dermot raised his hand to pacify him.

'Before you object, Minister, I am removing your posters for your own benefit as much as mine. Your image is inextricably linked with the country going down the toilet. The less your constituents see of you, the more likely they are to vote for you. The opposite is true of me. The people of Dublin West have not had the pleasure of meeting me. They need to see that I am a man of substance and considerable good looks. It will be a nice change for them to be represented by somebody handsome. Are we clear on that?'

'Certainly, Dermot. Ahem, we couldn't just leave up one or two of mine, could we? Just one even? I've always had posters … some lovely ones over the years.'

'I am sure you have, Minister,' Dermot said. He looked as though he was about to dismiss Mr Lenihan but he paused for a moment. 'Perhaps you are right, Minister. Perhaps we should leave up some of your posters. People need a focus for their anger. Yes. Change of plan. Leave up your posters but don't put mine anywhere near them. I want my posters put between Varadkar's and Burton's. I don't want any of your guilt by association. Have you got that?'

'Yes, Minister, I mean yes, Dermot,' said the Minister.

'Let's not get ahead of ourselves, Minister. There's still an election to win. Now get out of here. And pick up my new suit from Louis Copeland's before you go to the constituency.'

'Yes, sir.'

'One more thing, Minister,' Dermot shouted after him. 'Get me a footstool. Seán keeps fidgeting and it's making me uncomfortable. Seán, you may go.'

Seán Murphy, one of the few highly qualified economists in the Department of Finance, slowly got to his feet and shook his legs and hands to get rid of pins and needles. I had found him to be competent and diligent but he looked a beaten man now. 'Will there be anything else?' he asked wearily.

'From you?' said Dermot with a look of complete and utter disdain. 'What else could I possibly need from you?'

With that, a chastened Seán retreated to his desk. I felt honour-bound to stand up to Dermot over the way he had treated this high-ranking member of the Department.

'Dermot that really is an appalling way to treat anybody, never mind such a highly-qualified economist. I have been very impressed with Seán during my time here. He could really be of great assistance to you in sorting out Ireland's balance sheet.'

'Hah,' said Dermot. 'He's an economist. What would he know about anything?'

'You can't be serious?' I said.

'Deadly serious,' said Dermot. 'I've been managing finance ministers for many years and I have never met one who needed the opinion of an economist. An economist won't tell you how to increase your vote. They can keep their silly ideas about effective economic management for *The Afternoon Show*. I have to live in the real world.'

I was shocked by Dermot's comments. His dim view

of economists was, of course, appalling for a man in his position, but how on earth could we expect him to manage Ireland out of the crisis if he genuinely believed that he lived in the real world?

'What are you doing here anyway?' Dermot asked me.

'Where you go I go, you know that,' I told him.

'Even on the campaign?' he said. 'How interesting. Does Ajai know?'

'Ajai insisted,' I said.

'Did he indeed? Seán!' Dermot shouted. 'Get me a photographer and have a printer ready to do flyers.' Then he looked at me. He got up from the throne and slowly walked around me, making some sort of assessment. He turned and walked around me in the opposite direction.

'There's not much we can do about your pallor,' he said. 'You've obviously spent years hiding away in an office while your skin cried out for sunshine or solariums. You really will have to start taking better care of yourself. Even Joan Burton has a tan, for God's sake. Now is there anything about you that we can actually fix? You should at least get a haircut for the photographs.'

'What photographs?' I asked Dermot, as Julian, the hairdresser he had flown in from London, sat me down in a chair and tut-tutted over my hair.

'So dry!' Julian fussed. 'Haven't you ever heard of conditioner, darling? You'll need a hot oil treatment, and then we're going to frost your tips.'

'Just a short back and sides, please,' I said firmly.

'But you were meant to be a blonde! I can sense these

things – I'm spooky that way,' he told me as he flapped over my thinning hair.

'You should listen to Julian,' said Dermot. 'He got David Cameron into No. 10.'

Julian nodded sagely.

I glared at both of them.

'I don't want any treatments and I don't want frosted tips,' I said. 'I don't even know what they are.'

Julian looked hugely offended. 'I am an artist, not a common barber,' he said huffily.

'Just get your tips frosted,' said Dermot. 'You're not coming on the campaign looking like that and I don't want Julian pissed off before he does me.'

An hour later I smelled of ammonia and looked like I had been in a very gay car crash. Julian was so busy exclaiming his delight with the results that he was oblivious to the horrified look on my face. I decided not to offend his artistic sensibility again and instead went to the barbers on Baggot Street and got a No. 1 all over.

'You look like a moneylender's enforcer,' Dermot told me when I got back.

I thought that was at least a slight improvement.

'So what are these photographs?' I asked him again.

'Just normal baby-kissing, dog-petting campaign photographs,' he said.

'But I'm not running for election.'

'No,' said Dermot. 'But you are coming on the campaign trail and you can either stand there and look like the menace to the Irish way of life that you are, or you can be warm and friendly and mislead my voters into thinking that the IMF are nice and we should play ball with them. It's up to you. What do you think Ajai would want?'

'He'd want to know how much you're paying for your haircut,' I said.

Dermot waved a hand dismissively. 'Election expenses,' he said. 'And everyone's saying we need a haircut anyway! You should have seen Mary Harney's hairdressing bill. She went all the way to Florida to have it done. God, I liked her style. And as for Bertie's make up ... he wore more than Lily Savage, you know. Anyway, you have a decision to make. If you want to come on the campaign, you have to do the photographs.'

'OK,' I said. 'Warm and friendly. I'll do my best.'

'Fine,' said Dermot. 'But you look about as warm and friendly as Roy Keane.'

I spent that evening in Blanchardstown Shopping Centre getting my photograph taken with voters and curious kids. To my surprise Dermot had realised that the opportunity to meet an IMF man who was providing the cash to save the economy was a bigger draw than the chance to meet the senior civil servant who presided over the ruin of the economy. It never occurred to me that Dermot would be able to keep himself out of the limelight. Dermot was there, don't get me wrong, but he kept a relatively low profile.

But of course Dermot couldn't keep a low profile for long. I was quietly explaining to some poor woman whose minimum wage had been cut and who had lost two of her three part-time jobs that bad times don't last for ever and that a few years of austerity would see Ireland back on track. She told me she was having a tough time but that she was also up for the challenge.

'We can manage tough times Mr IMF,' she said. 'But can that shower of shites manage us back into good times?' she asked, pointing at Dermot.

'Well I can only speak from the perspective of the IMF,' I said, 'but from our point of view, Ireland is on the right track. You just need someone to keep it on track.'

'And that someone is me,' said Dermot with fake brightness. 'How do you do?' he asked the woman, keeping his hands firmly in his pocket in case she wanted to shake one of them.

'I don't know how I do at all,' she said. 'I barely get by.'

'I know exactly what you mean,' said Dermot. 'If it wasn't for my expenses I don't know when I would be able to dine out.'

'Dine out?' the woman said. 'Dine out? That about sums it up. You dine out while the rest of us are dying out.'

She turned to me then, clearly disgusted with Dermot. 'I'm sorry Mr IMF, I'd vote for you lot if ye ever decide to run but I'm not voting for that muppet,' she said and stormed off.

'Very good,' said Dermot. 'Another satisfied voter. I suppose I should have asked her to give her second preference to the Minister.'

'She was not a satisfied voter, Dermot,' I said. 'She was quite disgusted that you were comparing dining out on expenses to the difficulties she faces making ends meet.'

'Oh,' said Dermot. 'Well excuse me! We really are a nation of begrudgers.'

Dermot's campaign message was simple: government was far too important to be left in the hands of politicians. At first people were dismissive when they saw a candidate representing the civil service. Then they read his campaign leaflet, which claimed that all the prudent advice civil servants had given to ministers had been ignored for years. This argument actually resonated with people. Pretty much everyone in Ireland who isn't a public or civil servant is related to one and Dermot explained that they had been much maligned and scapegoated by politicians.

'The boom really would have got boomier if the politicians had continued to do what they were told,' Dermot told a voter. 'But with things going so well in the economy they started to believe that they were in some way responsible for the success. They became deluded and would listen to no-one. It was sad to watch – pathetic really.'

You could see that his message was getting through to people but Dermot invariably blew the advantage he was gaining by failing to empathise with people.

'I know how much you have suffered at the hands of politicians,' he told one woman whose interior design company had folded and who couldn't get the dole because she had been self-employed. 'But it was worse for me. I had to work for them.'

'I have no money for food,' she said. 'I haven't eaten

properly for weeks.'

Dermot looked at her with a tear in his eye. 'I know,' he said, as he handed her a sample tube of Fake Bake self tanning lotion from one of the salons that was sponsoring him, 'I know.'

Everyone, irrespective of age, gender or race, received a free tube of Fake Bake. 'Put that on,' Dermot would say. 'That will cheer you up and you won't feel so bad about not having any electricity.'

It was, of course, extraordinary to hand out Fake Bake to people whose life savings were lost, whose children had emigrated, whose houses were about to be repossessed, and expect them to vote for you. At first I thought there was a real possibility that Dermot would be publicly lynched. But the voters seemed to save their ire for what they called 'real politicians'. Some of them gave Dermot a hard time and threw the Fake Bake back at him in disgust, but mostly they seemed to consider him a harmless distraction. They were keen to debate the economy, the bailout and whether or not to default. Other candidates in the constituency engaged in animated debates on these issues but Dermot found such discussions boring beyond measure and refused to take part in them.

His campaign did nearly unravel when a young mother approached Dermot enthusiastically with her newborn baby in her outstretched arms. An RTÉ crew were filming the campaign and the woman obviously saw an opportunity to get on television. 'Kiss my beautiful baby, mister,' she said. Up to that moment Dermot had avoided physical contact with his constituents and their babies. The task of kissing, bouncing, burping and even changing babies had fallen to me. But on this occasion I couldn't get there in time and Dermot recoiled in utter horror as the baby's face neared his. The mother was understandably annoyed, but fortunately the film crew missed the moment and Dermot noticed his mistake and made up for it quickly. 'Kiss the baby,' he said to me and he instead took the mother by both hands and spoke to her privately for a few moments. I could see her attitude soften as he whispered in her ear. Her body leaned into him and she hung on his every word. A moment later they were back. She took her baby, smiled coquettishly at Dermot and was gone.

'I thought you had blown it there,' I said. 'What on earth did you say to her?'

'Oh, I explained that I was just back from a bunga bunga party in Rome and didn't want to risk passing on an unpleasant infection,' he said.

'She was OK with that?' I asked. I could scarcely believe it.

'More than OK,' he said. 'She promised me her first preference vote, although I had to promise her a year's supply of Fake Bake.'

'Wouldn't it be easier to just kiss the damn babies?' I asked him.

'Ugh,' he said. 'Who in their right mind would want to do that?'

He had a point.

If the voters were vaguely tolerant of Dermot, the politicians were not. To a man and woman they seemed outraged that a civil servant had 'crossed over'. One might have expected that the opposition would be happy that he was talking down Fianna Fáil and the Greens, saying they had refused to take advice and had often done the opposite to what Dermot had suggested. They were, however, not one bit happy. It was as though Dermot was breaking a sacred trust by running for office.

One evening when we were canvassing outside TK Maxx in Blanchardstown, it transpired that Joan Burton and her team had a similar plan to Dermot's. Dermot's hostility towards her was intense. This didn't surprise me after she and Michael Noonan had snubbed him when they came to the Department of Finance to discuss passing the Finance Bill. What surprised me was that she was clearly just as hostile towards Dermot.

'Ms Burton,' Dermot said icily. 'I will do everything in my power to ensure that you never work in the Department of Finance.'

'Really, Mr Mulhearn? Just like you do everything in your power to ensure that you never work in the Department of Finance?'

'Well I never,' said Dermot.

'Precisely,' said Ms Burton. 'At least you can go back to your life of genteel retirement in the Department after you fail to get elected. What about the poor people who have lost their livelihoods because of your ineptitude?'

I had never seen anyone speak to Dermot like this. She

would clearly be a breath of fresh air in the Department of Finance if she did get the position.

Dermot was not used to such treatment. He was speechless with indignation, but the situation was about to escalate.

'Is this bureaucrat haranguing you, Joan?' a voice behind us asked. We turned around to see another of the candidates, Joe Higgins of the Socialist Party.

'Look at you, you gilded lily,' he said to Dermot. 'You should get back to Merrion Street before you get hurt. She fights dirty, does that Burton one.'

'Who is "she" may I ask? The cat's mother?' Ms Burton broke in. A crowd had begun to gather as the politicians bickered.

'Oh, here we go,' said Mr Higgins.

'What do you mean "here we go"?' Ms Burton demanded. 'Was that a sexist "here we go"?'

Dermot, unfortunately, found his voice just as the crowd was growing in number.

'I am not going to sit here and be insulted by a woman and a socialite,' said Dermot.

'Who are you calling a woman?' Ms Burton demanded angrily.

'Who are you calling a socialite?' Mr Higgins demanded, sounding both angry and confused.

The crowd had swelled to about one hundred people.

'Well,' said Dermot, turning to face Ms Burton. 'You are not much of a woman with your politics and your economics and ... and ... your stupid hair ... and ...' He turned to face Higgins. 'As for you, you are not much of a social-ite. I eat in all the best restaurants and I've never seen you in any of them.'

Word spread about the free entertainment and the crowd grew still further. Dermot clearly thought he was winning the impromptu debate as each of his misguided comments was greeted with laughter and applause.

'How dare you?' shrieked Ms Burton. 'First, I'm a woman, then I'm not a woman. I don't know which is more insulting. The nerve of you.'

Dermot was about to respond but Mr Higgins interjected.

'And I'm not a socialite, you idiot; I'm a Socialist,' he said.

'Excuse me,' said Dermot, raising himself to his full height. He was clearly confident that on this subject he was something of an authority. 'I had the honour of work-ing with Bertie Ahern for many years. I know a socialist when I see one, and you sir are no socialist.'

Mr Higgins became apoplectic with rage. 'I am a socialist,' he insisted. 'How dare you put me in the same category as Bertie Ahern. He was a nihilist, not a socialist,'

'Whatever,' said Dermot and he smiled broadly at the crowd, mistaking their laughter for support.

'Well isn't it just typical of you all to be squabbling in the street like this,' a young man with a prudish manner and a self-satisfied smile said.

'Oh no, it's Varadkar,' said Ms Burton.

'What are you doing here? I thought you weren't a

people person,' said Mr Higgins.

'I am too a people person,' Mr Varadkar said petulantly.

'Prove it,' said Dermot, seeing an opportunity to paint Leo Varadkar in a bad light. 'Kiss that baby.'

Dermot was pointing to a red-faced, squalling baby with snot running over its lips and down its chin. Its own mother would be hard pressed to kiss it. Mr Varadkar looked momentarily horrified and a hush came over the crowd.

'I can't,' he said 'I have a cold.'

'Kiss the baby, Leo,' jeered Ms Burton.

'You kiss the baby,' Mr Varadkar replied.

'Why should I kiss the baby?' Ms Burton demanded. 'Is it because I'm a woman?'

'Not again,' said Mr Higgins. 'None of us should kiss the baby unless we can kiss all the babies.' His socialist principles obviously ran deep.

Dermot picked that moment to do the most surprising thing that I have ever seen him do. He bent down on one knee, produced a handkerchief from his suit pocket and gently wiped the baby's nose, mouth and chin. The baby stopped crying, looked up at Dermot and gurgled happily. Dermot then kissed the baby on the forehead. Cheers erupted from the crowd.

'You have a beautiful baby,' he said to the child's mother.

'Are ye joking?' the mother said. 'He's the spit of his father – as ugly as me arse.'

'Well,' said Dermot, as the crowd rolled around laughing. 'I am sure you have a beautiful arse too.'

Dermot's campaign had descended into farce but you

couldn't deny that the public enjoyed him. He was still out-side TK Maxx talking to voters two hours after his rivals had left. Several people I spoke to said they couldn't possibly give him their first preference but they would give him second or third. 'We all know we are going to have a Fine Gael government,' one man said. 'But we may as well have a bit of a laugh too.'

And Dermot wasn't a complete fool. As he posed for photographs, he continued to tell the voters how politicians were all the same but he was different. 'Lenihan and Cowen ignored my advice on the economy for nine years,' he told them. 'I guarantee you Michael Noonan will do exactly the same. You need me in the Dáil to make sure the politicians listen to the real experts.'

The next morning we were in the Harney Room in the Department of Finance and Dermot asked for a review of the key issues that we were encountering on the doorsteps. I scanned the list in my notebook.

'Emigration, jobs, the Universal Social Charge, the banks,' I said.

Dermot rolled his eyes to heaven. 'How dull,' he said. 'Have these people no lives?'

'They have difficult lives, Dermot,' I said.

'Who doesn't?' said Dermot. 'It took me half an hour this morning to decide what tie to wear with this shirt. I don't think I can face another day talking to those people.'

'Well it's the last day of campaigning Dermot, and you did very well with them yesterday,' I said.

'Yes, but at such a cost. I vomited for hours last night.

I still dry retch every time I think of that ugly little baby. I simply can't face any more of that.'

I spoke to Ajai later that day to give him an update on the campaign.

'What is Dermot promising?' Ajai asked. 'I hope he isn't making any promises he can't keep.'

'Well,' I said, 'some of them are going to be difficult to keep.'

'Oh no,' Ajai groaned. 'What has he done? He hasn't promised to default, has he? I don't think I could stand another tête-à-tête with Angela Merkel. She is grim.'

'No,' I reassured him. 'Nothing like that.'

'What is it then?' he demanded. 'Give me a straight answer.'

'Well, he's promised a lot of people an all-over fake tan that won't fade and won't leave any streaks.'

'Wow! A classic election promise.' Ajai said drily. 'Is he going to get any votes?'

'He'll get some – not many, but some,' I said. 'He might even squeeze through on transfers. People seem to like him.'

'What about the wider campaign?' Ajai asked. 'Is it going to be that Kenny guy? Are there any signs of unrest?'

'No, no signs of unrest. It will definitely be Kenny. It is just a question of whether he gets an overall majority. The most likely scenario is that he will be in with Labour,' I said.

'Labour? Are they left wing?' Ajai asked. 'What are their policies?'

'They don't seem to have any,' I said, 'but if they did they would be the same as Fine Gael's. All the main parties here are pretty much indistinguishable.'

    'So they'll be able to work together?

    'They should be.'

    'OK,' said Ajai. 'Keep me posted.'

— EIGHT —

ENDA AND HIS
IMAGINARY FRIEND
☆ ☆

Dermot surprised me by coming into the office on the morning of one of the most significant general elections in the history of the Irish State. He had taken annual leave for the duration of the campaign and seemed so bizarrely confident of winning a seat that I didn't expect to see him back in the Department of Finance.

But he was all business as he ushered the Chiefs of Staff of all the government departments into what had been the Harney Room but now bore a large plaque with the legend 'Senior Civil Servants' Recreation Room'.

'What do you want?' Dermot asked me as I hovered at the door, trying to see what was going on inside.

'Just seeing what's going on,' I said. 'It's part of my job description, you know. It's one of the terms and conditions of the bailout, if you recall?'

'Oh, come on in then,' Dermot said, 'if you must.'

I got quite a shock when I walked into the room. Everything had changed. A large mahogany table dominated the space and most of the Chiefs of Staff were seated around it. There were also seats positioned slightly behind each of the Chiefs where their deputies sat busily looking through notes. I saw that Liam was sitting in the position reserved for the Chief of Staff of the Department of Finance. He had a supercilious air about him that I hadn't noticed before. I was surprised and disappointed to see that he was dressed in an exquisite bespoke suit of the sort that Dermot favoured. 'Oh you're here,' he said when he noticed me. 'Haven't you got numbers to crunch?' Liam had never spoken to me like that before and I didn't like his tone. He looked self-satisfied and superior. My heart sank as I realised he reminded me of Dermot.

I noticed an empty seat at the top of the table. It was the throne.

'You may as well sit beside me,' Dermot said, and he pointed to an assistant's seat beside the throne.

'What's going on here?' I asked him.

'All will be revealed,' Dermot said with a flourish.

I took my seat. Dermot took his and he called the meeting to order. 'Gentlemen,' he said, for they were all men, 'allow me to welcome you to the first meeting of the new civil service Cabinet. Before we begin I would like us all to welcome Liam Horgan who is joining our ranks as Acting Chief of Staff of the Department of Finance. Welcome Liam to the hallowed ranks of the senior civil service. You have won the lottery of life.'

Liam was given a standing ovation by the assembled civil servants and looked far too pleased with himself for my liking. I feared his scruples had not made the journey to high office with him.

'Now,' said Dermot, 'as you all know we have always run this country, but from now on we shall do so without any interference from the Government.' Dermot paused for a moment as the room erupted into spontaneous applause. 'As you know I have taken the decision to cross over and I will soon be elected TD for Dublin West.'

Once again the assembled civil servants applauded.

I took the opportunity to whisper in Dermot's ear. 'You are heavily dependent on transfers,' I told him. 'It's a long shot that you'll get a seat.'

Dermot looked at me in astonishment. 'Don't be ridiculous,' he said. He turned to face his peers. 'Thank you, gentlemen,' he said, smiling broadly. He really was impervious to reality.

David Mulcahy, Chief of Staff of the Department of Justice, rose to address the room.

'If I may,' he said, 'I would like to express my gratitude and that of all your colleagues for the sacrifice you have made in becoming ... in becoming a ... [at this point Mr Mulcahy tried but failed to suppress a shudder as a brief expression of disgust crossed his face] ... in becoming a politician,' he sobbed.

Dermot raised his arms to placate his colleague.

'There, there, David,' he said soothingly. 'I appreciate the sentiment but we all know there was no choice. As you know, gentlemen, we civil servants have been ignored for too long. We have stood by stoically while our ministers consulted with so-called experts. We have seen the principles of good government ground underfoot as fashionable theories held sway. Gentlemen, the time has come for change. The time has come for us to put the civil service back at the heart of good government. From this day forth we will meet here in our Cabinet room to make the key decisions that will lead Ireland out of the darkness and into the light. Never forget, gentlemen, what's good for the civil service is good for the country.'

Dermot finished to rapturous applause, which gave me a moment to pick my jaw up off the floor.

'This is no less than a coup d'état,' I whispered to him urgently.

'That's right,' he answered proudly. 'It is a very Irish coup – the Government won't even know that it has happened.' He turned to face the room again. 'There is one further item on today's agenda if you would indulge me for another few moments, gentlemen?'

Slowly the room came to order as Dermot cleared his throat.

'Some of us have been here before but there are many in this room who will shortly be dealing with new ministers for the first time. And, given how long Fianna Fáil were in power, many of our new charges will be virgin ministers. This in itself is not a major problem. Yes, they will be eager, impulsive and full of themselves, but they always are for the first few weeks. Just remember that these people won't have any respect for the system that we hold dear. They have all made outlandish promises, and, initially, they will be intent on honouring them. Of course, we mustn't allow them, but don't fight them on this. Their conviction passes quickly in the face of our intransigence and rarely resurfaces. Any questions?'

David Mulcahy again addressed the gathering. 'Can we be clear about how our Cabinet will conduct its business here?' he asked Dermot.

'Certainly,' Dermot said. 'These meetings will enable the departments to cooperate in subverting the wishes of our ministers. You and I, David, shall guide our colleagues in leading their ministers to policy positions that we preordain. Purely in the interests of the country, of course.'

Liam raised his hand. 'What if we end up with a particularly bolshie minister like ... '

'Like Mr Noonan,' Dermot finished his sentence for him. 'Fear not, Liam. Every department has been issued with a broadcast quality video camera. If your minister is particularly zealous about something or you just want to stop him from rattling on, simply point the camera at him. It will distract him for hours. Even Mr Noonan.'

On that note Dermot called an end to the meeting and the various civil servants returned to their departments to while away time until it was reasonable to go for lunch. I went to my desk and prepared myself to break the news to Ajai. I was not looking forward to the call.

Ajai answered on the first ring.

'Have you ID'd the unsub?' he asked. I had forgotten

that the new season of *Criminal Minds* was airing stateside.

'Ehm.'

'Never mind,' said Ajai. 'What's going on with the election?'

'The turnout is high,' I said. 'Everything still points to a Fine Gael victory.'

'So why did you call? Have you any news?'

'Yes, Mr Chopra,' I said. 'How can I put this? Voting is continuing but Dermot has already formed a Government.'

'What?'

The controlled anger in Ajai's voice was chilling. Somewhere a central bank governor cut himself shaving.

'Well it's kind of like we supposed. He has formed a Cabinet of civil servants to run the country.'

'When did we suppose that?' Ajai asked tersely.

'Well, I told you he wanted to put the civil service back at the heart of government, didn't I?'

'You didn't say he was taking over the place. Is it going to fly?'

'To be honest I don't think the actual Government, when it is formed, will ever know that it is not the actual Government,' I said.

'And what about Dermot's Government? Will it meet the terms and conditions as set out in the Memorandum of Understanding?' Ajai asked.

'I can't say for sure, Mr Chopra, but it is far more likely to succeed than one that has to answer to the will of the people.'

'Let me think,' said Ajai. 'I presume you still have Dermot's ear?'

'Very much so,' I said.

'OK,' said Ajai. 'Stay close to him, be useful to him but don't become compromised. Be with him if his plan works. Don't be there if it doesn't.'

'Yes, Mr Chopra,' I said as though it were possible to follow those instructions.

The following morning I called Dermot to go to the count centre but he said it was far too early. 'There won't be any cameras there yet,' he said. 'We'll wander in after lunch. I'll probably be elected on the first count shortly after that.'

I couldn't get over his supreme confidence. It reminded me of the glossy advertisements for graceful living on the hoardings outside ghost apartment blocks.

So, after a pleasant lunch in Thornton's, we made our way to the count.

'I can't wait to see Moany Joany's face when I romp home,' Dermot said as we walked into the hall just in time to hear that Joan Burton had in fact romped home, easily winning the first seat. Dermot was almost pale with disappointment and Ms Burton couldn't hide her delight.

'Oh, Dermot,' she said. 'I hope I give you enough transfers to get you elected. It would be a service to the Department of Finance to remove you from it.'

'It will be the only service you ever do for the Department of Finance,' Dermot said coldly. Then he remembered his manners. 'Still, I suppose congratulations are in order for your remarkable achievement.'

'Remarkable? Why is it remarkable?' Ms Burton demanded. 'Is it because I'm a woman?'

Dermot brought his hand to his mouth to stifle a yawn and turned his back on Ms Burton to find that he was facing the Socialist Party candidate, Joe Higgins.

'I am surprised you bothered to turn up,' Mr Higgins said. 'You have nothing to offer the people of Dublin West, or, indeed, the people of Ireland.'

'I assure you that you are mistaken, Mr Higgins,' Dermot responded. 'It is your sieg heil nonsense that the people of Dublin West will reject.'

'That's National Socialism, you buffoon,' Mr Higgins said. 'I am not a Nazi, I am a Socialist and a worker.'

'A Socialist and a worker,' Dermot said. 'That's novel.'

Before an irate Mr Higgins could respond, another voice interjected. 'Is this a private party or can anyone join in?' Leo Varadkar asked.

'Fuck off, Leo!' Dermot, Mr Higgins and Ms Burton said in unison.

As I had expected, Dermot's first preference count was pitifully low but he did get a bounce once Ms Burton's surplus was distributed. The early signs were that the people of Dublin West were keeping their promise to give Dermot their second or third preference. It was as though they were hedging their bets in case the real politicians let them down. Dermot, however, could not hide his disappointment when Mr Varadkar was the second TD elected. 'They really should vet people before they give them a vote,' he said sniffily.

The bottom three candidates – an independent, a Green and the second Fianna Fáil candidate were then eliminated, and their transfers, although helpful to Dermot, actually propelled Joe Higgins to the Dáil after the third count. 'We need a dictatorship,' Dermot said. 'The vote is wasted on these commoners.'

On the next count a Sinn Féin and a Fine Gael candidate were eliminated, with their transfers narrowly getting Minister for Finance Brian Lenihan over the line. Dermot was devastated. He had assumed that Mr Lenihan would lose his seat. However, he did his best to conceal his disappointment. 'Congratulations, Mr Lenihan,' he said. 'You're the last of the Mohicans. The only Fianna Fáiler from Dublin remaining in the Dáil. We will have to try and organise a preservation order for you.'

With only one seat remaining, Dermot was neck and neck with the second Labour Party candidate, but he sneaked ahead on transfers and was deemed elected to the fifth seat although he did not reach the quota.

Dermot immediately forgot the ignominy of coming so close to failure as he was hoisted aloft by jubilant civil servants and paraded around the room.

'What will happen now in the Department?' I asked him. 'Will Liam be confirmed in your position?'

'God no,' said Dermot. 'I can take five years' leave of absence. Liam will keep my seat warm. He's always been terribly dreary but I think he's growing into the job. High office has a way of bringing out the gloss in people. He's next in line for promotion so he will get it eventually if I decide to stay in politics.'

I was about to ask Dermot what his plans were now that he had been elected but an intense, agitated RTÉ reporter actually pushed me out of the way and asked the question for me.

'This is CHARLIE BIRD asking Dermot Mulhearn to tell CHARLIE BIRD what his plans are,' the reporter, whose name appeared to be Charlie Bird, said rather loudly.

'Well, Charlie,' Dermot began.

'CHARLIE BIRD,' Charlie Bird corrected.

'My apologies,' said Dermot. 'Well, Charlie Bird, I intend to wait and see who is forming the new Government and I will then offer my assistance and expertise in the efficient management of that Government.'

'Can you tell CHARLIE BIRD what you will be seeking in return for your assistance and expertise?' Charlie Bird asked.

'Oh, nothing for me,' said Dermot.

'Oh, nothing for me, CHARLIE BIRD,' said Charlie Bird.

Dermot sighed. 'Nothing for me, Charlie Bird,' he said. 'But I would insist that the Government treats the civil service with the respect it deserves.

☆   ☆   ☆

I left Dermot and his civil servant friends to celebrate his victory and went back to the apartment. The weeks of campaigning had taken their toll and I fell asleep on the couch. When I awoke, Dermot was standing in front of me with Enda Kenny, who was sporting a large 'I am the Taoiseach' badge on his lapel.

'Meet the new Taoiseach,' Dermot said. 'He took a helicopter straight to Dublin from his constituency in Mayo just to shake your hand. Taoiseach, meet the man with the money.' Out of the side of his mouth Dermot then whispered to me: 'Actually, he came to Dublin to celebrate Fine Gael's victory but his TDs gave him the slip, so I took the opportunity to introduce him to my plans for the new Government.'

I was about to congratulate the new Taoiseach on his election victory when he turned his head to one side and said to someone who clearly wasn't there: 'Did you hear that, Paddy?' he said. 'He called me Taoiseach.'

I was utterly confused and looked to Dermot for guidance. 'How silly of me,' said Dermot. 'I forgot to introduce you to our Taoiseach's most trusted friend and adviser, Paddy.'

'Hello, Paddy,' I said uncertainly to the empty space beside the Taoiseach.

Mr Kenny was delighted. 'You can see him too!' he said, beaming. 'Some people say they can't see him.'

'Don't mind them spoofers,' said Dermot. 'Of course they can see him. Isn't he a fine figure of a man? But he would be nothing without you, Taoiseach. You are clearly the boss in the relationship.'

'Do you think so?' Mr Kenny asked.

'Definitely,' said Dermot.

'Excuse us, Taoiseach,' I said, 'while Dermot and I get you a cup of tea.'

'Don't forget Paddy,' the Taoiseach said.

'No, Taoiseach,' I assured him, 'we won't forget Paddy. How could we?'

'What the hell is going on?' I asked Dermot as soon as I closed the kitchen door behind us.

'Nothing much,' said Dermot with a shrug. 'Our new Taoiseach has an imaginary friend.'

'An imaginary friend?' I was in shock. 'The leader of your country has an imaginary friend. Is he supposed to be an improvement on Brian Cowen?'

Dermot shrugged again. 'Well, he's certainly more presentable. He'll probably forget about Paddy now that he's Taoiseach,' he said. 'He just needed him in the difficult years when even his own party couldn't stand him. The first fifty-nine years of his life have been terribly lonely. He was never invited to sleepovers when he was a child, and now they don't even want him at the Fine Gael victory party. Paddy is a great comfort to him.'

I was speechless and I had absolutely no idea what to tell Ajai about this. We returned to the living room with four mugs of tea for the three of us.

'Paddy wants to know what's going on,' Mr Kenny said as we sat down.

'Well, Taoiseach,' said Dermot. 'I suppose we should prepare you for your meeting with Mr Gilmore to negotiate the formation of the Government. It won't be easy.'

'He's a very pushy little man,' said Mr Kenny.

'He is,' said Dermot, 'but you are well able for him. Remember he wanted to be Taoiseach but you are Taoiseach; you have the badge and everything.'

Every time Dermot called him Taoiseach, Mr Kenny smiled broadly and winked at Paddy.

'The first thing he will do,' said Dermot, 'is try to get you to make Joan Burton Minister for Finance.'

'Michael Noonan has to be Minister for Finance,' Mr Kenny said. 'He made me promise him that.'

'How did he make you?' asked Dermot.

'He told me to,' said Mr Kenny. Then he leaned forward and whispered, as though afraid that Mr Noonan would somehow hear him: 'He said he'd eat my liver with some fava beans and a nice chianti.'

'Ugh,' said Dermot, 'I hate fava beans. Don't pay him any attention, Taoiseach. He's a scary man, but we will protect you.'

'He thinks he's the boss of me,' said Mr Kenny.

'Well he's not, Taoiseach. You are the boss,' said Dermot. 'Now listen closely; this is what I want you to do. You need to appoint two Ministers for Finance – Michael Noonan and one of the Labour lads. The two of them will fight all the time and leave you and Paddy to run the country in peace.'

Mr Kenny laughed when Dermot mentioned him running the country. 'Noonan and Burton?' Mr Kenny asked.

Dermot looked troubled. 'That is up to you, Taoiseach. You're the boss,' he said doubtfully. 'It is entirely your decision. But the media will blame you if Ms Burton doesn't work out.'

'What do you think?' Mr Kenny asked me. He looked worried.

'I met her a few times during the campaign,' I said. 'She struck me as a very capable woman.'

Dermot shook his head from side to side. 'A capable woman,' he said ruefully. 'Is there anything more difficult to manage than a capable woman, Taoiseach? And a member of the Labour Party too. You would have no peace, no peace at all.'

The Taoiseach looked troubled. 'She can be very mean,' he said.

'Exactly,' said Dermot. 'You know, if you gave the job to someone else in Labour, someone like that pipsqueak Howlin, you could cause a rift within their ranks. It will be much easier for you to govern if Labour are fighting among themselves.'

'I see,' said the Taoiseach tentatively. 'Maybe I should appoint Brendan Howlin then.'

'That's a great idea, Taoiseach,' said Dermot. 'How clever of you to think of it all by yourself.'

The Taoiseach giggled nervously. 'Paddy helped me,' he said.

'Paddy is a great adviser,' said Dermot.

'Now,' said Mr Kenny, and he looked meaningfully at Dermot. 'Do you want to be a minister?'

'Oh no, Taoiseach,' said Dermot. 'I have important work to do. Anyway, I'm not a member of Fine Gael.'

'Oh dear,' Mr Kenny said. He looked troubled. 'You're not in Labour are you?'

'God forbid,' said Dermot. 'No, I am not a member of any party and I am not seeking a ministry. I would be very happy, however, to advise you on how to deal with the civil service in the difficult times that lie ahead. I have much experience in that field and I know how they think.'

'Hmm,' said Mr Kenny. 'Do they know you know how they think?'

'Yes, Taoiseach, they know I know how they think but they think I think like them.'

'I see,' said the Taoiseach. 'And do you think like them?'

'Oh no, Taoiseach,' Dermot smiled. 'I think like us.'

'Very well,' said the Taoiseach. 'I will appoint you to the post of Special Adviser to the Taoiseach. What about you?' Mr Kenny asked me. 'Would you like a job? Paddy could do with an assistant.'

'I already have a job, thank you, Taoiseach,' I said. 'But I will happily assist you and, erm, Paddy in any way I can to make the bailout work.'

☆   ☆   ☆

For the next few days I was in constant attendance on Dermot while he was in constant attendance on Mr Kenny. Although he was supposed to advise the Taoiseach only on matters relating to the civil service he had quickly gained Mr Kenny's complete confidence and was consulted on absolutely everything. This didn't impress Mr Kenny's Fine Gael colleagues or his potential coalition partners.

'What is he doing here?' the Labour Party leader, Eamon Gilmore, asked when he walked into the room for the first post-election meeting between the two party leaders. He was referring to Dermot who was standing at the Taoiseach's shoulder. Neither Mr Gilmore nor any of the other politicians who entered the room in the days that followed paid any attention to me. All I did was pay the bills.

'He's my adviser,' said the Taoiseach firmly.

'I thought Paddy was your adviser,' Mr Gilmore said sarcastically.

'Paddy is my friend,' the Taoiseach said defensively.

'Yes,' said Mr Gilmore, 'of course he is. Listen, I have accepted, against my better judgement, that Paddy goes where you go but I must draw the line at Mr Mulhearn. He has to go. You can't have him as an adviser. He's part of the problem, not the solution.'

'Dermot said you'd say that,' said the Taoiseach.

'But Enda,' the red-faced and clearly frustrated Labour leader began.

'It's Taoiseach Enda,' Mr Kenny interrupted.

'You're not Taoiseach yet,' Mr Gilmore reminded him.

'And you're not in government yet, Mr Gilmore,' Dermot broke in with a smile.

'Very well,' said Mr Gilmore. 'Taoiseach Enda it is.'

The Taoiseach smiled at Paddy and then at Dermot, who smiled back.

'I have grave reservations about Mr Mulhearn advising you,' Mr Gilmore went on. 'He is tainted by his time in the Department of Finance and the dreadful decisions that were made there.'

'They were Brian Lenihan's decisions,' said Mr Kenny. 'Dermot did his best but Lenihan wouldn't listen to him; Dermot told me so. We must listen to Dermot so that we have full civil service support for our government.'

'If you say so,' said Mr Gilmore wearily. 'But Joan isn't going to like it one bit.'

'Ah yes, speaking of Joan,' said Mr Kenny.

'Hmm, Joan,' said Dermot, almost grinning.

'What about Joan?' asked Mr Gilmore.

'May I say, Mr Gilmore,' Dermot said. 'That it takes a big man to allow her to speak as frankly about your leadership as she did on the doorsteps of Dublin West during the campaign.'

'What are you talking about?' Mr Gilmore asked.

'I am just saying that I admire the way you allowed her to openly discuss your leadership qualities with her constituents,' Dermot continued.

This struck me as strange as I had been with Dermot throughout the campaign and I had never heard Ms Burton do anything of the kind.

'She did what?' asked an increasingly agitated Mr Gilmore.

Mr Kenny interrupted. 'We need someone who can introduce reform without ruffling too many feathers.'

'Joan ruffles feathers,' said Dermot.

'Yes, Eamon,' said Mr Kenny. 'She's terrible for ruffling feathers. See how she has ruffled yours?'

'Well where can we put Joan, then?' Mr Gilmore asked. We have to put her somewhere.'

'It's a pity there isn't a Department of Home Economics,' said the Taoiseach.

Everybody roared with laughter except me. I had to ask Dermot what was so funny.

'Home Economics for Moany Joan,' he said, almost crying with laughter. 'You know, cooking and dressmaking and crochet.'

'But that's absurd,' I said. 'Ms Burton is a highly capable woman.'

A deafening and awkward silence descended on the room. I had clearly spoken out of turn. The atmosphere reminded me of the Boxing Day debacle.

'The Department of Social Protection has a big budget,' said the Taoiseach, breaking the silence.

'Indeed,' said Dermot. 'Tough decisions will have to be made there if we don't meet our obligations under the Memorandum of Understanding with the IMF. Social welfare might have to be cut. It needs a minister who isn't afraid to be deeply unpopular.'

I was surprised Dermot knew anything about the Memorandum of Understanding, but I kept my mouth shut.

'Joan would be very good there,' Mr Kenny and Mr Gilmore said in unison.

'So, that's settled,' said Mr Gilmore. 'Now who will I

put in Finance with Noonan?'

'What about that little fellow who's negotiating for ye?' said Mr Kenny. 'The one who's even smaller than you.'

'Howlin?' said Mr Gilmore. 'I'll have you know he is much smaller than me.'

'Let's put him in Finance. Noonan might not even notice him.'

They agreed that Mr Howlin would be appointed to the new position of Minister for Public Expenditure and Reform.

Then the two party leaders set about sharing out the other Cabinet positions.

'I have to give something big to Bruton,' the Taoiseach said. 'All the kids in the party like him for some reason.'

'Why not give him Enterprise?' said Mr Gilmore.

'In the middle of a recession that is only going to get worse? That's a great idea! Fair play to you, Eamon,' the Taoiseach replied, delighted with the idea.

'No bother, Taoiseach,' said Mr Gilmore. 'But what will I do with Rabbitte? I have a pain in me arse with him.'

'Why not give him Communications?' Dermot suggested. 'He never shuts up anyway.'

'Right,' said the Taoiseach, 'how about Varadkar for Transport?'

'Is he even old enough to drive?' asked Mr Gilmore.

'If he's accompanied by an adult,' Dermot volunteered.

'That leaves Frances Fitzgerald,' the Taoiseach said, scratching his head. 'Another woman.'

The Taoiseach, Mr Gilmore and Dermot looked

blankly at each other for a moment as they considered what to do with Ms Fitzgerald.

Suddenly the Taoiseach stood up. 'Ah lads,' he said. 'We've been missing the obvious. We'll make her Minister for Children. Women love children.'

'Right,' said the Taoiseach. 'All that remains is to decide what position to give Paddy.'

'Ah come off it, Taoiseach, you can't appoint Paddy to a post,' Mr Gilmore said.

The Taoiseach looked hurt and offended. 'Why not, Mr Gilmore?' he asked. 'I might make him Tánaiste instead of you.'

'You could all right,' said Mr Gilmore angrily. 'If he existed.'

Mr Kenny looked extremely upset. 'Paddy exists,' he cried. 'Paddy is real.'

Fortunately Mr Gilmore realised his mistake and made a good recovery. 'I meant if he existed as a TD. If only Paddy had a seat, he would make a marvellous minister.'

We were about to leave work later that evening when the new Minister for Finance, Michael Noonan, stormed into the Taoiseach's office in a fury. He was not happy with having to share his department with Brendan Howlin. Mr Kenny looked scared and he kept a chair between him and the Finance Minister, just in case Mr Noonan attacked. 'What do you think you're doing cutting my department in half?' he demanded as he attempted to grab the Taoiseach by the scruff of the neck.

'I can do what I like. I'm the Taoiseach,' said Mr Kenny nervously, pointing to his badge.

'Yes,' said Mr Noonan. 'You are the Taoiseach. But watch your step, Enda, because I've had Taoisigh bigger than you for breakfast.'

Something about the way he said it made me think he meant it literally.

Mr Noonan turned to leave, glaring at Dermot and me as he walked to the door. He stopped in front of Dermot, fixed him with an unsettling gaze and suddenly did the gnawing action of a rat like Hannibal Lecter in *The Silence of the Lambs*. 'Don't cross me, bucko,' he said, poking Dermot in the chest. Poor Dermot needed sedatives after that and the Taoiseach decided that the security arrangements for his office should be reviewed.

A couple of days later Dermot and Mr Kenny were discussing the appointment of junior ministers.

'Fifteen sounds about right, don't you think?' said Dermot.

'But I promised the people I would only appoint twelve,' said the Taoiseach.

'Exactly,' said Dermot. 'That's why you must appoint fifteen.'

'I don't understand,' said Mr Kenny.

'Don't worry, Taoiseach. Allow me to explain,' said Dermot. 'These are difficult times are they not?'

The Taoiseach looked at Dermot for guidance and then guessed the right answer. 'Eh, yes,' he said.

'And in these difficult times the public's expectations must be kept in check,' Dermot continued. 'You mustn't give the people false hope, Taoiseach. If you start keeping election promises now they will expect you to honour all of your promises. They will expect you to achieve all of your goals. What sort of government would do that, Taoiseach?'

'A good government?' This time the Taoiseach guessed incorrectly.

'No, Taoiseach,' said Dermot. 'A fantasy government would do that. The government of Cloud Cuckoo Land. It has never happened and it never will.'

'I see,' said the Taoiseach.

'Good,' said Dermot. 'Taoiseach, your role is to manage the expectations of the people of Ireland. It is vital that you keep those expectations low. You can do it Taoiseach. You are good at it. After all no one ever thought you would amount to anything, did they?'

'No,' said the Taoiseach. 'They didn't. Apart from Paddy. Paddy always believed in me.

NINE

PADDY WANTS A
BETTER BAILOUT

✩ ✩ ✩ ✩ ✩ ✩ ✩ ✩ ✩ ✩ ✩ ✩ ✩ ✩ ✩ ✩ ✩ ✩

The two new Ministers for Finance couldn't have been more different. The actual Finance Minister, Michael Noonan, or Dr Lecter as Dermot called him, arrived first. Of course we had already had dealings with Michael Noonan in the Taoiseach's office but his formal arrival in the Department of Finance was a more managed affair. An advance nurse came to the office first to make sure our slippers had arrived and that we were wearing them. Fine Gael HQ had informed us that we would have to wear slippers in the office at all times as Mr Noonan hated to be woken unexpectedly. So it was no surprise that he was asleep when he was wheeled in by two more nurses.

'Are all phones on silent?' one of the nurses whispered. Liam, Dermot and I nodded in unison. Dermot had persuaded the new Taoiseach that he should return to the Department of Finance to help the new ministers acclimatise. Although Dermot had had no time for Liam in the past, they now appeared to be almost joined at the hip. The pair seemed to be constantly conspiring and giggling.

All mobile phones were indeed on silent and the land-lines had been fitted with lights that flashed for incoming calls.

'If anything should cause him to wake suddenly, don't loosen his ties until he calms down. Usually a nice cup of tea with one sugar and some buttered Rich Tea biscuits will soothe him. He often drifts off again after that,' one of the nurses told Liam.

Liam looked at the slumbering figure of the Minister for Finance as his head lolled to one side and he drib-bled saliva on his shoulder. He was snoring steadily but, strangely, his eyes were wide open.

'Jaysus, his eyes are open. How do you know he's asleep?' Liam asked the nurse nervously.

'Oh, don't mind his eyes,' the nurse said. 'They're always open. There are two ways to know if he is awake. If Mr Noonan wakes calmly, his snoring gradually becomes quite erratic until he wakes and asks for biscuits. If he wakes suddenly, he will be confused and agitated and he will try to kill you.'

Minister Howlin couldn't have been a greater contrast. He came skipping into the room, sat in a swivel chair and spun around several times, his short legs swinging freely as he did so. 'Have you a camera phone?' he asked me. 'Take a picture of me.'

'Shh,' we all said in unison but it was too late. Mr Noonan sat upright in his chair, fixed his eyes on Mr Howlin, put his hands out as though to strangle him and said: 'I am going to kill you, ya little upstart.'

'You're after waking him up,' Dermot remonstrated with Mr Howlin, but the new minister couldn't have cared less.

'Somebody give the old fool a biscuit,' he said.

Liam approached Mr Noonan tentatively with two buttered Rich Tea biscuits and a cup of tea. Mr Noonan glared at him but grudgingly accepted the offering.

There was a general air of relief in the room at how well Liam's first dealings with the new minister had gone but it was short lived. Liam was walking over to Dermot and me with a broad triumphant smile when Mr Noonan's cup hit him on the side of the head, cutting his ear. 'This is not butter, ya fucking eejit,' Mr Noonan bellowed.

I got Liam a tissue to stem the flow of blood from his ear as Dermot attempted to placate Mr Noonan. 'Now Minister,' Dermot said. 'These are difficult times. That spread has 5 per cent butter. That is the best we can afford in the current circumstances.'

'Lenihan had Jammie Dodgers. I want proper butter,' Mr Noonan bellowed. 'I bet he had his biscuits buttered on both sides too.'

'Those were different times, Mr Noonan. Mr Lenihan lived beyond the country's means. I am sure you don't want to do that, do you?' Dermot responded soothingly.

'I want proper bu ... ' Mr Noonan began, but he abruptly started snoring as he fell asleep as suddenly as he had woken.

Dermot sent a visibly shaken Liam for a lie down and then turned his attention to Mr Howlin, the Minister for Public Expenditure and Reform.

'So, Mr Howlin, you are the Minister for Spending,' he said. 'How nice for you. Weir's have the summer Rolex range in if you are interested.'

'Spending and Reform,' Mr Howlin corrected as he spun ever faster on his chair. 'I spend but you pay. Your civil servants won't like that.'

'Ah, Minister,' he said. 'I am quite sure my erstwhile colleagues will be only delighted to be reformed. Will it hurt? Should they fast for twenty-four hours beforehand?'

'You may be sure it will hurt,' Mr Howlin said. 'But you shouldn't be here, should you? You're a TD now, shouldn't you be on a junket somewhere?'

'The junkets will have to wait Minister. I am helping the Taoiseach adapt to the pressures of government. One of the things he has kindly asked me to do is to act as liaison between you and the civil servants you are so eager to reform. Won't that be nice?'

Minister Howlin stood on his seat, puffed up his chest and rose to his full height. 'You'd better not interfere with my reforms, Dermot Mulhearn. Don't stand in the way of Hurricane Howlin!'

'I wouldn't dream of it, Minister,' Dermot assured him. 'Please don't huff and puff and blow our house down.'

Mollified, Minister Howlin sat back in his seat and attempted to reach the desk beside it.

'Does this seat not go any higher?' the Minister asked as

he desperately struggled to reach the desk.

'That's not your seat or your desk, Minister,' Dermot said. 'When we found out that both you and Minister Noonan would be joining us, we commissioned matching furniture for you. Yours is the same as his in every detail but three quarters the size.'

Dermot and I left the Minister skipping around the office, stealing pens and generally making a nuisance of himself, and went to check on Liam's well-being. He was resting in the Senior Civil Servants' Recreation Room.

'That was quite alarming,' Liam said. 'The new minister is volatile, isn't he?'

'Oh, you should have seen Bertie's rages,' said Dermot. 'They were a force of nature, truly awesome to behold. Noonan is nothing by comparison.'

'Well I wish you were still here to handle him,' Liam said.

Dermot shot Liam a look of disdain. 'Pull yourself together, Liam,' he said. 'To all intents and purposes you are the Chief of Staff of the Department of Finance. It is time you started acting like one. Michael Noonan will not present us with any problems. All you have to do is gain the trust of his nurses and get them to adjust his medications as you see fit. That shouldn't be too much of a chore now, should it?'

'No, Dermot,' said Liam.

'That's more like it,' said Dermot. 'Now start acting like a Chief of Staff. Go shopping. Have a nice long lunch somewhere. Order yourself a new car.'

'Yes, sir,' said Liam.

As Liam opened the door of the Recreation Room to leave, Minister Howlin fell flat on his face on the floor in front of us. He had clearly been jumping up in an attempt to reach the door handle.

'What's going on in here?' the Minister asked as he picked himself up off the ground. 'What sort of conspiring and conniving are ye up to?'

'Now, Minister,' Dermot said. 'This room is for senior civil servants only. I am afraid you can't come in. The unions wouldn't like it. You won't be able to reform the civil service if they are all out on strike.'

'I'll do what I like,' Mr Howlin said as he left. 'If you have a room like this, I want one too.'

'Of course, Minister,' Liam said. 'I shall immediately put the construction of a ministerial recreation room out to tender.'

'It's him we have to watch, not Noonan,' Dermot said, thinking aloud. 'That little shit actually thinks he is going to reform the civil service. That is what happens when you give someone a job they're not expecting to get – unrealistic expectations.'

The following morning Dermot and I flew to Brussels with the Taoiseach for a meeting of the European Council. The Taoiseach was still very wary of Mr Noonan and made Dermot promise not to tell him or Mr Howlin that we were travelling to Brussels with him. 'The less they know the better,' the Taoiseach said. 'Noonan is terrible for holding a grudge.'

Dermot and the Taoiseach spent the entire flight in earnest conversation. I heard snippets of the discussion as I sat immediately behind them with Paddy.

'You have to show them who's the boss, Taoiseach,' I heard Dermot saying.

'I do?' asked the Taoiseach.

'You do,' Dermot replied.

'Dermot,' said the Taoiseach, 'who is the boss?'

'You're the boss Taoiseach,' Dermot said patiently.

'Oh yes,' said the Taoiseach. 'I keep forgetting. It's all happened so fast.' He turned to face behind him and winked at Paddy. 'Paddy has to remind me several times a day, don't you Paddy? I'd be lost without you.'

'You're a great man, Paddy,' Dermot said to the empty seat beside me. 'So, Taoiseach, do you know what to say?'

The Taoiseach looked out the window for a moment, composed his thoughts and replied. 'We want to burn the bondholders,' he said. 'We have inherited a mess that is not of our making. We want the EU and the ECB to lower the interest rate on the bailout.'

'Very good, Taoiseach,' said Dermot.

'And Paddy can't come in?' the Taoiseach asked.

'It would be better if he didn't,' said Dermot. 'It would be better if you don't mention him at all, Taoiseach. Keep things simple for Monsieur Sarkozy. He is a simple man.'

President Nicolas Sarkozy of France and Chancellor Angela Merkel of Germany sought the Taoiseach out at the summit to offer their congratulations on his triumph in the Irish general election.

'Enda, mon brave, congratulations on becoming Taoiseach of your bankrupt little country. You must be very proud,' President Sarkozy said generously.

The Taoiseach patted the diminutive French president on the head. 'By God, you're small,' he said. 'I have a toy Finance Minister at home who is bigger than you – and he's tiny.'

Before Mr Sarkozy could respond to the unexpected insult, Mr Kenny turned his attention to the German Chancellor. 'Ms Merkel,' he said with all the confidence he could muster, 'Paddy wants a better bailout.'

Dermot raised his eyebrows and glanced at me uneasily. Ms Merkel exchanged a bemused look with Mr Sarkozy. It seemed Mr Kenny's nerves had got the better of him. Faced with the daunting task of standing up to the German and French leaders he had forgotten Dermot's advice and reverted to relying on Paddy. Instead of being firm he was being cocky and offensive.

'Paddy can - how do you say? - fuck off,' said Monsieur Sarkozy. 'And you can fuck off with him.'

Ms Merkel was the calmer of the two European leaders. 'We have given you billions and angered our electorates by doing so,' she said. 'If Paddy wants a better bailout, Paddy has to give something in return.'

The Taoiseach paused for a moment to consult with his imaginary friend. 'As a Mayo man I pride myself on being a canny negotiator,' he said eventually. 'What do you want?'

'Your corporate tax rate,' Ms Merkel replied.

The Taoiseach considered his options. 'Would you settle for Achill Island?' he asked.

'Don't be ridiculous, Enda,' Ms Merkel said. 'We already have all the good bits of Achill.'

'I promised the good people of Ireland that I would never surrender our corporate tax rate,' the Taoiseach said. 'It is very dear to the hearts of the Irish people. Ever since Fionn MacCumhaill hunted on the plains of Royal Meath we have been proud of our ability to facilitate tax dodging by international companies. It is part of who we are.'

'Enda, who cares about Fionn MacCumhaill? The fact is you're broke.' Ms Merkel said. 'I am sure the good people of Ireland are no different from the good people of Germany or France – they don't believe their politicians' promises, do they?'

'I suppose not, Angela,' the Taoiseach said. 'May I call you Angela?'

'No, Enda, you may not,' said Ms Merkel, and she turned her back to Mr Kenny.

We had a post-mortem on the flight back to Dublin.

'Well that didn't go according to plan, did it?' Dermot said.

'There was a plan?' I asked.

'Don't be a bore,' said Dermot. 'Of course there was a plan. Enda was supposed to be resolute and not for turning, like Mrs Thatcher.'

'I think you may have been expecting a bit much from him,' I said as I glanced at the Taoiseach who had confided to me on the way to the airport in Brussels that he wasn't sure if he wanted to be Taoiseach any more.

'Well what do you think we should have done, clever clogs?' Dermot asked me.

I sighed. How often had I tried to get him to read the Memorandum of Understanding before it was signed? 'All you can do now is soldier on,' I said. 'If you are fortunate, and the Portuguese are not, Portugal will apply for a bailout.' There's strength in numbers. You never know, they might even employ someone who can negotiate for you as well as them.'

'Don't be bitchy,' said Dermot. 'You might be right though. It might be time for Portugal to get a bailout.'

Morale was sinking ever lower in the Department since Minister Howlin's arrival. He somehow managed to offend every civil servant he came across. He blatantly stole snacks off people's desks and openly threatened the staff with reform if they so much as looked at him. Several clerical officers took to stooping when they walked past him, as they feared being reformed if they appeared taller than the Minister.

Dermot was right – Mr Noonan turned out to be much more manageable than Mr Howlin. In general, he was very subdued, although he did have an annoying habit of throwing chalk at people he thought were talking in class. On one occasion he caught me on the cheek with a piece of chalk as I discussed the quarterly review on Skype with Ajai.

'What the hell was that?' Ajai asked.

'Oh, it's just the Finance Minister,' I replied. 'He was a teacher before he became a politician and apparently he used to throw chalk at pupils to get their attention.'

Ajai looked momentarily confused. 'So,' he said. 'We're going to be there next week for the review. What should I expect to find?'

'It's a mixed bag, Mr Chopra,' I said. 'They have been quite enthusiastic about cutting services but they somehow generate costs while doing it.'

'How is that possible?' Ajai looked irritated.

'I don't know; it's like a gift they have, a sleight of hand that introduces two costs while cutting one. By the time you track down the offending cost and eliminate it they have generated two more. Two weeks ago they agreed to move a section of the Revenue Commissioners to cheaper offices. It created a saving of €230,000 a year. Then they gave all the staff involved €10,000 each and three days' extra annual leave for the inconvenience of having to move to an office around the corner. I have it all documented. I think they just find it difficult to change old habits.'

'They are going to have to,' Ajai said.

'I know,' I said. 'That's not the real problem though, Mr Chopra.'

'What's the real problem?'

'They remain completely fixated on saving the banks to the detriment of everything else. I cannot get Dermot or Liam to pay any attention when I ask them to focus on improving competition and changing work practices.'

'So they don't mind what becomes of the wider economy?' Ajai asked.

'Not one bit, sir,' I said. 'As long as their own privileges are not removed they don't give a damn about anything else.'

'I see,' Ajai said. 'It sounds as though we're going to have to save Ireland from the Irish.'

☆   ☆   ☆

Dermot was on the phone as soon as he got up the next morning. He had a sense of urgency about him, which made me think he was probably planning a social function. But I was wrong. 'Pack a bag,' he said. 'We have a dinner engagement in Lisbon.'

'Not another dinner, Dermot. Ajai will be here next week. We should be focussing on how to introduce a property tax, not dining out in Portugal.'

'Saddling people with a property tax when they can't pay their mortgages isn't going to get you your money back,' Dermot said. 'We have to think bigger than that.'

He phoned Liam and got him to arrange the tickets. At the airport, I went to the bathroom and came back to find Dermot paying for an €8,000 watch.

'Nice, isn't it?' he said cheerfully.

'Lovely,' I said. 'I see Sinéad gave you your credit card back.'

'Fat chance of that,' said Dermot. 'Anyway I cancelled it and got myself some new ones. This is on the Department's card. It's an investment in Ireland's future.'

'That's a ridiculous extravagance, Dermot,' I said. 'And you don't need a watch to know Ireland's time is up. The writing is on the wall.'

'Don't be so wet,' he said. 'There's all to play for yet.'

After checking into our hotel we took a taxi to Dermot's mystery engagement at a restaurant called Tavares. Dioguo Abalada, Dermot's opposite number in the Portuguese Department of Finance, greeted us on our arrival. He was a handsome man, dark and swarthy, and he evidently had similar taste to Dermot when it came to the finer things in life. His suit was beautifully tailored, and a big, brilliant diamond shone from the centre of his tiepin.

'So good to see you, Dermot. It has been too long,' he said, embracing Dermot warmly.

'It has, Dioguo,' Dermot said. 'We must organise another Scottish golfing holiday.'

'That would be delightful,' Mr Abalada said as he turned his attention to me. 'This must be your friend from the IMF. He looks as though he hasn't two euros to rub together.'

'Tell me about it,' Dermot sighed. 'He buys his suits in bargain stores.' The two civil servants shuddered simultaneously. 'Will they let him into the restaurant, do you think?'

Mr Abalada nodded. 'Don't worry,' he said. 'They know me well here. I will get them to make an exception.'

As we entered the restaurant Mr Abalada had a discreet word with the maître d', who looked over at me and shrugged. 'Everything is OK,' Mr Abalada said. 'Don't worry.'

The maître d' showed us to our table and went to get us aperitifs on the house. While he was gone Mr Abalada told us something about the restaurant. 'This is Lisbon's oldest restaurant,' he said. 'It opened in 1784. It has had many great chefs but none greater than our current host, Portugal's youngest Michelin-starred chef, José Avillez.

'He trained in the kitchens of masters such as Ferran Adrià, Alain Ducasse and Eric Frechon and is now a master himself. For you gentlemen I recommend starting with the traditional Portuguese sopa alentejana, which is a soup concocted of garlic, bread and egg.'

'That sounds very nice,' I said.

Dermot put two fingers down his throat. 'Sounds vom, Dioguo,' Dermot said. 'Isn't there any foie gras?'

Mr Abalada and Dermot laughed hysterically for a few moments.

'You are right, Dermot, it does sound vom. Why don't we all have sautéed foie gras to start followed by lobster with mushrooms and chestnuts, or "The Civil Servant's Supper" as they call it here?'

The two civil servants chatted amicably as I took in the opulent décor of mirrored walls with gold trim and crystal chandeliers. The setting suited my dining companions down to the ground.

'So,' said Mr Abalada as we sipped brandy at the end of our meal. 'I suppose you don't get to do this too often now that the IMF are footing the bill.'

'On the contrary, my dear Dioguo. Life in Ireland is very much as it was before the IMF came in. If anything it is better. We never have to worry about where the money is coming from,' he said.

'So you would recommend an IMF bailout?'

'Wholeheartedly and unreservedly,' said Dermot. 'It's the best thing we've ever done.'

'Hmm,' said Mr Abalada, 'you surprise me.'

Dermot surprised me too. As ever I wasn't entirely sure what he was up to but I supposed it wasn't necessarily a bad thing to be giving a good review of the IMF to Mr Abalada when Portugal would almost certainly be our next client.

'Excuse me, gentlemen,' I said. 'I must use the bathroom.'

When I returned, the bill had been settled and Dermot and Mr Abalada were embracing at the door. As I approached them Mr Abalada turned to me with outstretched arms. I couldn't help but notice that he was wearing the watch Dermot had bought in Dublin.

'My dear friend from the IMF,' Mr Abalada said as he embraced me, 'thank you so much for the beautiful watch. It is just what I was looking for.'

We were back at the hotel before Dermot agreed to explain what he had done.

'It's no big deal,' he said. 'I just had the watch engraved "For Dioguo, looking forward to working with you, the IMF".'

'You did what?' I could feel my blood pressure rising.

'Come on,' Dermot said. 'I had to. You said yourself that we needed Portugal in the mix to improve our Ts & Cs.

Dioguo is going to talk to his colleagues about persuading their political masters to opt for a bailout. Portugal gets a bailout and Ireland gets a lower interest rate – everyone's a winner!'

'How the hell am I a winner? I didn't tell you to frame the IMF by bribing a civil servant to persuade his government to take an IMF bailout,' I screamed at him.

'Steady on,' said Dermot. 'I didn't really see it like that.'

'You didn't see it like that?' I said. 'What the hell am I going to tell Ajai?'

Dermot laughed. 'I wouldn't tell him anything if I were you,' he said.

'Since when have you cared about the bailout or the interest rates anyway, Dermot?' I asked him. 'You weren't interested when you had a chance to negotiate it.'

'Believe me I am not interested now either,' Dermot said. 'It's all terribly dreary but I am trying to do right by the Department of Finance. We have been getting a very bad press recently. Last week I went to Patrick Guilbaud's and was given a table by the toilets. If sorting out this bloody bail-out is the price I have to pay for a bit of respect, then so be it.'

It was several days before I spoke to Dermot again. They were hectic days as the Department gradually got used to its new ministers. Mr Noonan's unpredictable behaviour modified and he slept for almost the entire day. I suspected Liam had come to an arrangement with one of his nurses about increasing his medication levels.

Mr Howlin was a different story. His extraordinary capacity to rub people up the wrong way became more and more pronounced and he quickly established himself as a hate figure among the staff.

The civil servants took a lot of abuse from him but it was inevitable that someone would eventually snap under the pressure. It happened early one morning, when two clerical officers had had enough and decided to take revenge on him. They grabbed Mr Howlin from behind, hoisted him up and hung him on the coat rack outside our office. The Minister was livid. 'When I am finished reforming you even your own mothers won't recognise you,' he screamed.

I tried to help him down but was intercepted by the staff's union representative, who informed me that I did not have the right to interfere with the Minister and that my actions could lead to a diplomatic incident. It was next to impossible to get any work done for the rest of the afternoon with the Minister screaming abuse at anyone who passed him. Thankfully, Dermot dropped by in the evening and lifted him down.

'I suppose I ought to thank you,' Mr Howlin said.

'Don't mention it,' said Dermot with a smile. 'Us politicians must stick together.'

The bank stress testers from BlackRock Solutions were also rubbing Department of Finance staff up the wrong way. The consultants had been called in to convince Ireland's paymasters in Europe that the estimate of how many billions would be needed to save Ireland's banks was accurate. Of course, they were used to consultants round the Department, but these ones were, as one of the clerical officers said, a cut above butter. 'They have calculators and everything,' he said bitterly.

It didn't help that the consultants openly mocked the Department of Finance officials.

'You guys sure made one hell of a mess of managing your economy,' one of them said to Liam. 'Didn't any of you ever play Monopoly?'

'Actually, we prefer Texas Hold'em,' Liam replied sniffily.

The stress tests eventually revealed that the Irish banks would need a further €24 billion to help them cope with potential losses. The Ministers for Finance were hoping to bring this information to the EU and haggle for a better interest rate. But they hadn't reckoned on Dermot's trip to Portugal. Just as Minister Noonan was preparing his pitch to the EU and ECB, the news broke that Portugal had applied for a bailout. Ireland's problems were off the agenda as Europe's Finance Ministers focused on their latest problem.

Dermot was furious. 'We did everything right,' he said. 'We hired proper consultants and did proper tests and they still won't listen to us.'

'They will, Dermot,' I said. 'They just have to absorb the Portuguese situation first.'

'You said it would help us if Portugal had a bailout,' he said, with a venomous edge to his voice.

'It probably will, Dermot,' I said. 'Be patient.'

'Be patient, he says. Be patient! We do horrible stress tests that upset everybody and cost us a fortune, we get Portugal to apply for a bailout and what thanks do we get? None!' he said. 'A big fat zero! In fact, worse than that, the bloody ECB put up interest rates. Roddy Doyle was right – the Irish are the blacks of Europe.'

'You really should stop with the self-pity, Dermot,' I said. 'It is making matters worse instead of better. You need to keep taking action and prove to Europe and to Ajai that you are putting your house in order.'

'What a bore,' said Dermot. 'I have to go. I'm late for a meeting of the real Cabinet.'

Two hours later Dermot and I were in the so-called Senior Civil Servants' Recreation Room among the assembled Chiefs of Staff of the Irish civil service. Everyone was congratulating Dermot on his coup in getting Portugal to apply for a bailout when Liam called the meeting to order.

'Gentlemen,' he said, 'our miniature Minister for Finance has been causing quite a bit of grief. For a man who had neither a job nor the prospect of one only a few weeks ago, he has shown himself to be irritatingly determined to make his mark on Irish history. I am sorry to say that Minister Howlin is determined to wreck the Irish civil service and we are all that stands in his way.'

A gasp echoed around the room.

'What information do you have?' Dermot asked Liam.

'The Minister came to me this morning and said he was going to carry out a root and branch reform of the civil service,' Liam said with a tear in his eye.

I was disappointed to see him so opposed to reform.

'But we knew that,' Dermot said. 'I told you that.'

'It was the way he said it,' said Liam. 'There was a demonic look in his eye. He means to crush us, gentlemen.'

Again a shudder went around the room. It was as though the most cosseted men in Ireland had suddenly been touched by the icy finger of the recession.

Dermot stood to address the room. 'Gentlemen, gentlemen,' he said, 'we will still be here long after Mr Howlin is gone. After all, he cannot reform the civil service without the civil servants.'

Almost immediately the tension in the room dissipated as the men realised that they were essential to the success of the Minister's plans.

'This is what we must do,' Dermot said. 'The Minister knows I have the Taoiseach's ear, so he doesn't trust me. Liam, you must gain his trust.'

'But how?' said Liam.

'Nothing could be simpler,' said Dermot. 'You are just an acting Chief of Staff. We can use that to our advantage. Warn the Minister that the Chiefs of Staff of each department are determined to thwart his plans for reform. He can't work alone. He needs someone to trust. That someone will be you.'

The room again erupted into spontaneous applause as it became clear that Dermot, through Liam, would take control of civil service reform, thus ensuring that there wouldn't actually be any reform. I was disappointed with Liam and told him as much when the meeting ended.

'I thought better of you Liam,' I said. 'I thought you would realise the importance of reforming the civil service.'

'What ever made you think that?' Liam asked.

'The conversations we had,' I said. 'You made it clear you didn't approve of the way Dermot did things.'

'I don't remember that,' said Liam, with a broad grin as he flicked a speck of dust from the sleeve of his designer suit jacket. 'No, I don't remember that at all.'

— TEN —

WE ARE WHERE WE ARE
☆ ☆

I was sitting across from Ajai in the Merrion Hotel eating a simple breakfast of a croissant and coffee. I envied him staying here now. It seemed so clean, so well ordered, so normal. My apartment was the opposite since Dermot had moved in. Ajai and his European counterparts had returned to Ireland to begin a two-week review of Ireland's progress. It was the first quarterly review – the first of many. The first review is usually a gentle affair. We recognise that a country and its people need time to absorb the reality that the IMF is now in charge. At the first review you are never where you said you would be but always where we expected you to be. Unlike the Irish, we have done this before.

'So,' said Ajai, 'what's it like working with the new Government?'

'Pretty much the same as working with the old Government, Mr Chopra,' I said. 'The faces are new but the level of incompetence is similar. Mr Kenny has turned out to be the lightweight you described on the plane when we first came here.'

Ajai smiled coldly. 'I saw he got his balls handed to him by Merkel and Sarkozy,' he said.

'Yes, sir,' I said. 'He went out to Europe full of bluster about burning the bondholders and came back with his tail between his legs. The Government have been sulking ever since.'

'Sulking?' said Ajai. 'They are like children.'

'Yes,' I said, 'like children with special needs.'

Ajai shook his head. 'Merkel and Sarkozy,' he sighed. 'If I didn't know better I would say they are determined to bring down the Euro. They keep driving broken countries into our embrace, all to save banks that should have been let go to the wall. No one who lent cheap money to the Irish is blameless.'

I sipped my coffee and said nothing.

'So Dermot's star has risen?' Ajai said eventually.

'Yes,' I said. 'He has manoeuvred himself into a position of considerable power. The Taoiseach doesn't turn around without consulting him – he thinks they're best friends for ever. And now he has the Civil Service Cabinet answering to him. Nothing happens here without Dermot's say so.'

'And you and he still have a good relationship?'

'Yes, sir.'

'Good. So what will he do with his power? Will it cause us problems?' Ajai asked.

I cast my mind back an hour to when I had left Dermot at the apartment. He was playing *Red Dead Redemption* with fellow independent TDs Ming Flanagan and Mick Wallace. The three new TDs bonded on the first day of the new Dáil, finding that they shared a similarly low opinion of politicians. They have been hanging out together ever since and seem to have an alarming amount of free time. Like Arts students avoiding their lectures, they spend their time watching *Charlie's Angels* re-runs and playing on the Xbox. They each see something of themselves in *Red Dead Redemption*'s anti-hero John Marston, a one-time outlaw who hunts down his former gang members for the government after they have taken his wife and son hostage.

'Isn't that just typical of a government?' Ming said in disgust. 'I've had to stop smoking cannabis in case they use it as an excuse to intimidate my family.'

'I don't care what the government do, I'm not changing my shirt,' Mick Wallace said heroically.

'I asked you a question,' Ajai said sternly.

'Sorry, Mr Chopra. It's early days but I don't think Dermot is going to rock the boat. He knows where the money is coming from. He'll make sure the Taoiseach sticks to the terms and conditions – as long as they don't affect Dermot's terms and conditions.' *And until the €85 billion is spent*, I thought to myself.

'Good,' said Ajai. 'You have done well with Dermot. Have you any concerns?'

'Yes, Mr Chopra, I am worried about one thing in particular. All the government and civil service seem to care about is saving the banks. They remain bizarrely proud of them despite the fact that they have brought the country to its knees. This obsession with the banks consumes them and leaves them no time for getting the real economy back up and running. And if they don't do that, I don't see how they will ever be able to pay us back. To be honest, I'm not sure they have any intention of paying us back.'

'They will pay us back,' said Ajai with certainty. 'But that's another day's work. Now what is this business of having two Finance Ministers instead of one?'

'It's really only one-and-a-half, Mr Chopra. Minister Howlin is very small,' I said, trying to lighten the mood.

Ajai looked at me blankly. He's not big on jokes. 'They're supposed to be reducing the public service numbers,' he said flatly.

'Yes, sir,' I said. 'Reducing public service numbers is Mr Howlin's responsibility. Mr Noonan has all the other Finance Department duties.'

Ajai shook his head. 'He's reducing public service numbers by creating a job for himself,' he said.

'I am afraid so,' I said. 'Sir? Erm … I wonder is there any chance that I could be reassigned now? Perhaps I could go to Portugal? Is there something I could be doing at Head Office?'

Ajai studied me for a moment. 'Why?' he asked.

'I think I have done all I can here, Mr Chopra,' I said. 'And to be honest I need a break. I need to get back to the States to sort out this neck injury. I don't want to see any more Irish doctors. No one should have to do that.'

A look of complete disdain crossed Ajai's face and he made no attempt to hide it. 'Pull yourself together,' he said.

'We'll discuss your situation after the review.'

The forensic team spent ten days examining Ireland's performance under the Memorandum of Understanding. Finally, Ajai was ready to sit down with the new government and explain to them exactly what they had to do for the next few months. 'So,' Ajai said as we walked to the Department of Finance, 'if I let them reverse the cut in the minimum wage and allow this non-event of a jobs initiative, they will be happy?'

'They'll think they've won the lottery,' I told him.

We sat down at a large conference table in a meeting room at the Department and waited for the Taoiseach, ministers and assorted hangers-on.

Ajai was clearly taken aback when Minister Noonan was wheeled into the room by a nurse. Ajai opened his mouth to speak but I stopped him just in time. 'Shhh!' I said. 'The Minister gets very aggressive if woken suddenly.'

A moment later Public Expenditure and Reform Minister Brendan Howlin swaggered into the room with a coterie of officials. He walked over to Ajai, who had stood up to shake his hand. The Minister stepped up onto a box placed on the ground by one of his entourage. Then he put his arm around Ajai and got another official to take a photograph of them. 'This will go on the wall in my office,' he said, smiling broadly at the camera. Ajai looked disturbed.

As soon as the photograph was taken, Mr Howlin's friendly manner abruptly changed.

'You think you're so big, don't you, Mr Chopra,' he sneered. 'Well you're not so big now!' With that, to my utter astonishment, Mr Howlin kicked Ajai in the shin.

'Ow,' yelped Ajai. As the leader of the IMF delegation bent to nurse his leg, Mr Howlin stood over him and ran his hand from the top of his own head down to the stooping Ajai. 'See!' he said triumphantly, indicating Ajai's diminished height. 'I'm the king of the castle!'

All the commotion had woken Minister Noonan, who was now straining at his ties and screaming for biscuits.

It took Ajai a moment to regain his composure. 'Who the hell is that little man?' he said through clenched teeth, colour rising in his face.

'That's Brendan Howlin, the mini Finance Minister,' I said.

'Did he really just kick me in the shin?'

'I believe he did, Mr Chopra.'

'Let's just get this meeting underway, before somebody gets seriously hurt,' he said tersely, glaring malevolently at Mr Howlin.

Tea and buttered Rich Tea biscuits were brought into the room by a young civil servant. There was also a jug of Miwadi for Mr Howlin. Minister Noonan fixed his gaze on the refreshments and followed their progress towards the table without blinking.

Dermot arrived with the Taoiseach in tow and strode straight up to Ajai and embraced him like a long-lost friend. Ajai stood stiffly with his arms at his sides. 'So good to have you back, Ajai,' Dermot said. 'I hope we can play a round at the K Club before you leave. They're crying out for green fees at the moment.'

'I should hope they are,' said Ajai. 'I don't have time for golf. Shall we get started?'

'Yes let's,' said Dermot.

Everyone but the Taoiseach took their seats. Mr Kenny was looking around the table in an agitated manner, a panicked expression growing on his face.

'This won't do,' he said. 'It won't do at all.'

'What is the matter, Taoiseach?' Ajai asked him. 'We are trying to get some work done here.'

'There is nowhere for Paddy to sit,' the Taoiseach replied. 'We can't have the meeting without Paddy. Paddy likes to know what the story is.'

Perhaps if Mr Howlin had not just kicked Ajai in the shin, he would have dealt with the issue of the Taoiseach's imaginary friend in a gentler manner. Instead, an exasperated Ajai stood up, removed his glasses and said, 'Mr Kenny, I'm afraid I have to put a stop to this nonsense now. Paddy does not exist. Deal with it and move on.'

Mr Kenny looked nervously around the room.

'I told you he didn't exist, you half-wit,' Mr Noonan said, apparently in his sleep.

Mr Howlin sniggered into his Miwadi.

'What do you mean?' Mr Kenny eventually asked Ajai.

'Paddy is not real. He does not exist,' Ajai repeated.

'Like the economy?' the Taoiseach asked Ajai in a timid voice.

'No, Mr Kenny,' Ajai shook his head. 'Not like the

economy. The economy does exist. It is just very, very small. Paddy is not small. Paddy does not exist. He never did. He is a figment of your imagination.'

The Taoiseach looked at me, then he looked back at Ajai. He looked at Dermot. He was slack-jawed and stupefied. 'I have an imagination?' he said, shattered and bemused. He sank to the floor and curled up in a foetal position. Dermot went to comfort Mr Kenny.

'There, there, Taoiseach. There, there,' he said in a soothing voice.

The Taoiseach rocked back and forth in Dermot's arms.

'Paddy isn't real. I have an imagination,' he said, apparently trying to make sense of a new reality.

We were doing our best to ignore the spectacle before us but it was like trying to tear your eyes away from a car crash.

'It's OK, Taoiseach,' Dermot said. 'Having an imagination is fun. You'll see. Now, I have an important meeting here, Taoiseach, so I need you to go out onto Merrion Street and count how many blue cars you see between now and when it gets dark.'

'Blue cars,' the Taoiseach said brightly. Then he frowned again. 'What if I don't see any blue cars?'

'Then you can use your imagination, Taoiseach,' Dermot said with a smile. He turned to face Ajai. 'Now let's get down to business, Mr Chopra,' he said.

'Biscuits,' said Mr Noonan out of the blue. 'I want biscuits.'

'Give him his biscuits,' Ajai said, 'and let's get on with this.'

The nurse gave Mr Noonan a buttered Rich Tea and he instantly fell into a trance-like reverie.

'Gentlemen,' said Ajai, addressing Dermot rather than the two ministers, 'I am pleased to say that your initial efforts in meeting the terms and conditions in the Memorandum of Understanding have been successful. We have a long way to go but we are on track. I have spent the last few days going through the books for the first three months. We now know where we stand. We need to negotiate where we are going.'

'We want to reverse the cut in the minimum wage and run a jobs initiative,' Mr Noonan read from a Post-it note, spitting biscuit crumbs across the table as he did so.

Ajai looked at the Minister with distaste and brushed the crumbs from his suit jacket. 'That's fine, Mr Noonan,' he said. 'We always acknowledged that there would be room for you to change a few commas and put your own stamp on the Memorandum of Understanding. Tell me about this jobs initiative.'

'We're going to create jobs,' Mr Howlin butted in. 'And you can't stop us.'

'I see,' said Ajai. 'And just how do you propose to create these jobs?'

'We're going to announce them of course,' Mr Howlin said. 'How else would you do it?'

'You can't create jobs just by announcing them,' Ajai said.

'Yes you can,' said Mr Howlin triumphantly. 'That's how I got my job.'

Ajai shook his head. 'As far as I am concerned you can have your jobs initiative,' he said. 'But it has to be cost neutral.'

Mr Noonan slammed his hand down on the table. 'I want biscuits at the launch,' he said.

Ajai looked at me over his glasses. 'It will have to be cost neutral – apart from two packets of biscuits,' he conceded.

I made a note of this so it could be added to the Memorandum of Understanding.

'Now, how are you going to pay for reversing the cut in the minimum wage? The money has to come from somewhere.'

'I will get it from the civil service,' Mr Howlin said excitedly. 'No one can stand up to me.'

'Don't mind him,' Dermot said to Ajai. 'We'll get the money from the health service. If people are genuinely sick they won't notice.'

'As you wish, Mr Mulhearn,' Ajai said.

'How dare you ignore me! I will reform both of you,' Mr Howlin said angrily.

Ajai and Dermot yawned simultaneously.

'We want a reduction in the interest rate,' Mr Noonan said, still looking at his Post-it note.

Ajai shrugged. 'That's an issue for the EU,' he said. 'Take it up with them.'

'Enda tried,' Mr Noonan said. 'The bastards wouldn't listen to him.'

'They think they're great, with their tans and their

functioning economies,' said Mr Howlin bitterly.

'Well there is nothing I can do about that, I'm afraid,' Ajai told them.

Mr Noonan fixed Ajai with a chilling stare. 'Listen here, bucko. I want a reduction in the interest rate and I want it before the bell rings for hometime,' he said. Then he looked down at his empty mug. 'And I want a fresh pot of tea.'

Dermot told a civil servant to bring more tea and biscuits.

'I'll see what I can do, Mr Noonan,' Ajai said wearily. 'Now, to the matter at hand ... Mr Noonan ... Mr Noonan ...'

The Finance Minister was fast asleep.

'He always has a nap around this time,' I told Ajai, who was looking at the Minister in exasperation. Mr Howlin was busy spinning around on his chair.

'Get these clowns out of here,' Ajai said. 'I want to talk to Mr Mulhearn alone.'

'Come on, gentlemen,' Dermot said. 'You can go and tell the media about your great success in renegotiating the bailout. What a triumph!'

Dermot ushered the ministers to the pre-arranged press conference where the media were gathering, eager to hear how they had got on.

Ajai turned to me. 'What about the new guy, the new Dermot? Where is he?'

I cleared my throat. 'Err ... he's not back from Augusta yet,' I said warily.

'Augusta? What the hell is he doing in Augusta?' Ajai asked.

'He went to the Masters on Saturday. Some Irish guy called McIlroy was leading it. He went out on the government jet.'

'To a golf tournament? While we are carrying out the first quarterly review of the bailout? That sounds like something Dermot would do. I thought the new Dermot was better than the old Dermot.'

'The new Dermot was better than the old Dermot,' I said.

'But?'

'But when he got Dermot's job the new Dermot started acting like the old Dermot. He might as well be Dermot now.'

Ajai put his head in his hands. Just then Dermot came back into the room. Liam was with him. His skin was now the same orange hue as Dermot's and he carried himself with a new arrogance.

'Sorry to be late, Ajai,' Liam said. 'We had to queue to land. Not much point in having a government jet when you need permission to land, is there?'

Ajai looked at Liam. 'Who is this?' he asked.

'This is Liam,' said Dermot good-naturedly, 'the new me, as it were.'

'Good,' said Ajai. 'I have been wanting to talk to you. Who is in charge of the financial institutions now? I want to know why they are still handing out bonuses. You have years of austerity to sell to your people. I don't understand why the people who destroyed your country are being given bonuses.'

'There's no one in charge of the banks,' said Liam with a smirk. 'Why would there be?'

'No one is in charge of them?' Ajai said. 'How is that possible?'

'They have no money left, Ajai,' said Liam as if he was talking to an idiot. 'It would be an irresponsible waste of money to have anyone in charge of them now. We couldn't justify it. We have to watch every penny in the current circumstances.'

Ajai was dumbfounded.

I think Dermot felt that this would be a good time to change the subject. 'Ajai, as you may know, in order to best manage our situation, my senior civil servant colleagues and I have formed a ... Cabinet, for want of a better word.'

'I am aware of your venture, Mr Mulhearn. Not only do you have two Finance Ministers, but you also have two Cabinets. This must be what is meant by an Irish solution to an Irish problem.'

'Perhaps we could have two bailouts as well,' Dermot suggested.

'Perhaps not,' said Ajai. 'What did you want to tell me about this Cabinet of yours?'

'It's like this, Ajai. We have a problem with the Memorandum of Understanding.'

'I see,' said Ajai. 'What might that be?'

'Simply put, it's not very *understanding*,' Dermot said. 'I mean to say it attacks the legal profession, the medical profession, pharmacists, politicians. These people are the very fabric of our society. These are people who cannot afford to be poor. They wouldn't know where to start. Our surgeons and barristers, like our politicians and civil servants, are among the best paid in the world. They are a source of great pride to the nation. Would you leave us with nothing to be proud of?'

'We don't want them to be poor,' Ajai attempted to reason with him. 'We just want them to settle for a little less in the interest of the common good.'

'Less is poor,' Dermot said with a shudder.

'Listen,' said Ajai. 'The IMF couldn't care less at the end of the day. If you want certain sections of society to retain all their privileges, then the poor will have to get poorer.'

'That's a great solution, Ajai,' said Dermot, writing it down. 'Thanks for that.'

That afternoon Ajai and our EU and ECB colleagues gave a press conference at which they said Ireland was on track in keeping to the conditions of the bailout. As Ajai and I returned to the Merrion Hotel from the press conference we passed the Shelbourne Hotel, where a fire sale of repossessed Irish properties was being held. There was such interest in it that the hotel could not contain the crowd and people were actually bidding for properties on the street. Cars had pulled up in the middle of the road and their drivers were shouting out bids to the auctioneers. In the middle of the crowd one man was shouting louder and becoming even more frenzied than the others as he waved his cheque book in the air, bidding on every single lot. It was Dermot. Elsewhere in the crowd I spotted other senior civil servants and government ministers bidding excitedly.

As soon as Dermot saw us he made his way through the melee to greet us. 'Isn't this great?' he said. 'I've bought two apartments already. They're going for a song. A few more of these sales and we'll be back on our feet. We won't need your bailout at all.'

'This is not very prudent of you, Mr Mulhearn,' Ajai said. 'I'd say your property market has a long way to go before it bottoms out.'

'Don't be so negative, Ajai,' Dermot said, as he bid on yet another apartment. 'There are loads of new TDs I can rent out these apartments to. They're as safe as houses.'

Ajai looked at me and checked his watch. 'I have to go,' he said. 'I'm due in Portugal.'

'What about me, Mr Chopra?' I asked. 'Can I go too?'

Ajai pointed at Dermot, who was back in the throng bidding on more properties. 'And leave him in charge?' he said. 'Are you mad?'

THE STORY CONTINUES ...

Follow the Eighty-five Billion Euro Man on Twitter:
@IMFDublinDiary